Chapter One

Raina woke with a start. Darkness surrounded her causing her heart to pound with dread. Never had she been unable to not see in the dark with her vampire and shifter heritage, nighttime was her friend. She pulled the soft comforter up with shaking hands, listening to the quietness of the room. "It was just a dream," she whispered, but it had seemed too real. Flicking the lamp on, she shrieked as a tall imposing figure jumped on top of her.

"Hush little girl. We don't want to wake the entire castle now do we?" Black eyes flashed red, the raspy tone of his voice sent a shiver of fear down her spine.

"What do you want? How did you get in here?" Her father was the Vampire King, and she knew without a doubt he didn't let this being into their home.

A snake like tongue came out of the being's mouth. She froze, hoping he didn't plan to touch her with it.

"If you come with me and don't say a word or make a sound, I will make sure nothing happens to your precious family. However, if you put up a fight, I'll become worse than the beast under your bed you've always feared," he hissed the words.

She tried to control her alarm at the knowledge he had of her and her family, and even more of her dreams or more aptly, nightmares. "Where are you taking me?"

Fingers tipped with blade like talons gripped around her throat, cutting off her oxygen and slicing into her skin at the same time. "Master wants you. I was sent to bring you to him. By the way," he paused. "This might hurt a little."

Pain exploded through every fiber of her, from her head to her toes. Fire burned through her veins like lava flowing out of a recently erupted volcano. Before she could wish for death, which she'd never thought she'd do, darkness consumed her once again. Her last images before losing consciousness were of her parents and twin brothers Damien and Lucas. How she wished she could hold them one last time. If she could have reached out to them, she knew they'd have saved her. The mental block the demon had surrounded her with kept her from all those she loved. Now, with her life flashing before her eyes, she hoped they knew how much she loved them, and that they were safe.

The next time she woke, Raina was sure she was dead, only the oppressing heat couldn't be where her next life would begin, she wasn't meant to go to hell. Sitting up, the room spun as her stomach lurched. "Oh god, I'm going to be sick," she groaned.

"I wouldn't advise that. Master doesn't like his chosen to be flawed."

Hearing the grating voice let her know she wasn't dead. That at least gave her hope. She blinked her eyes open, taking in the surroundings and wished she hadn't. Red rock walls with black furniture was everywhere. Sweat poured down her face and body, soaking her nightgown to her skin. Oh, shit, she realized with a start all she wore was a tiny slip of satin.

The beast who stole her from her bed raised his brows. "You'll be wearing a lot less when Master gets here."

"Why?" Hating the quiver in her voice, she swallowed the lump in her throat.

"He has plans for you." His red gaze looked her up and down. "I've no clue why. You look too human for my tastes." And she hated the way he made his words sound like a snake was hissing. Thank fuck she looked *too human* for his tastes. The black horns on top of his head along with the green tint to his skin made her skin crawl. Again, she caught the hatred in his gaze, and thought he was reading her mind.

Her brothers had tried to ingrain in her the need to keep her mind protected from intrusions, but she never had a reason to be so on guard. Now she pushed him out with ease, making sure nothing and no one could read what she didn't want them to.

After her mind was secure, she moderated her body temperature, instantly cooling her overheated flesh. Instinctively she reached out on the familial path, trying to reach her father, or brothers. The ability was blocked, sending her to the black ground, blood oozed out of her nose from the agony of trying. Dry heaves wracked her frame.

"I told you not to make a sound or try to reach out to your family. Did I not?" Black talons lifted her chin.

"You didn't say I couldn't once we were here," she gasped. On her hands and knees, Raina was sure the monster squatting down to her level was getting a hell of a show through the gap at the top of her gown, but she couldn't gather the energy to pull herself up.

He shook his head, the horns growing straight instead of curving. "Nobody disobeys me." He pinched her chin between his fingers.

She tried not to flinch at the new pain shooting through her. Didn't he say his Master didn't want her damaged?

"Please let me go. I won't tell a soul." The scent of her fear and blood flooded her senses.

She was lifted up with seeming ease, one hand wrapped around her throat, the other pulled back in a fist ready to pummel her. "The only souls to tell, don't care."

The sound of a door opening had the beast dropping her to the ground, her fast reflexes kept her from injury.

"Yo, Yomy, what you got there?"

"None of your business, Creed. Leave before Master gets here."

Creed. Raina tried to see who the owner of the delicious voice was. She rolled the name around in her head as her wolf raised its head and wanted to howl. She felt her canines drop, and wanted to push the being named Yomy out of her way to get to the newcomer. What kind of name is that any way? Yo and my put together.

"You silly boy. Why don't you run along like the good puppy you are, and leave this morsel for me to handle?" The deep baritone suggested he was more than happy to make Yomy do as he said.

The demon stood in front of Raina, blocking her view. "My job is not complete."

A tall dark haired man came into view. His black slacks and black top made him look like a debonair business man. He had to be at least six and a half feet tall. Surely he couldn't be human, especially since she was sure they were no longer on Earth.

Her wolf didn't care what he was, the hussy. Raina stood on her bare feet, trying to control her inner beast.

Creed flicked his fingers. "Go now and I will not hurt you. Much," he growled.

Oh, yeah, her wolf liked the sound of his voice.

"Just because you are the Master's bastard son, doesn't give you any right to order me around."

Shit, she ordered her wolf to calm down. No way in hell was she wanting a deranged kidnapper's son.

"Yomy, Yomy, do you never learn? I am more than just his bastard. I am *the bastard*."

One minute the demon who'd stolen her away was in front of her, the next he was flying across the room. Raina jumped back until the scorching wall held her up, staying as far away from the battling duo as possible. Shit! She'd watched her brothers and her father's elite soldiers fight from afar, but nothing had prepared her for the battle in front of her. Neither being caring that she watched them try to kill each other, and that was exactly what they were trying to do. Right before her eyes, the man named Creed grew even larger. His smooth tan skin became a startling red. Horns similar to the ones on top of Yomy's head grew from his own, only larger, and sharper looking. The black things gleamed in the overhead light as he became what she'd envisioned the devil himself would look like, only he still appeared a beautiful man. Her wolf still wanted him.

Blood splattered the walls from the many gashes inflicted by Creed, yet he appeared to be playing with the other demon. Raina eased toward the door she'd seen, hoping she'd find a way out. If she got away from Yomy and his blocks, maybe she could contact her dad or brothers. She didn't think she'd survive whatever Master, or the one named Creed had planned for her. Scratch that, she knew she wouldn't survive. That was probably their intention.

The door opened to a dark hall, the stench of decaying flesh hit her when she stepped out. Quietly, she shut the door and looked at the three tunnels. Each one was pitch black, but with her enhanced vision she was able to see beings lurking down all of them. With no other recourse she opened her mind, praying she could connect with her family. A sense of loss threatened to swamp her until she felt a light touch on the familial path, one she'd feared her ability to connect with again had been severed until that moment.

"Who is this?"

Tears blinded her for a moment at the deep baritone of her father, his anger seeping through to her.

"I asked who this was. If you don't answer me, I will make you wish you'd not disturbed me and my family."

The authority in his demand made her blink. Did they not know she was missing? Couldn't he tell it was her? *"This is Raina, Daddy."*

Proud she didn't come across as breathless as she'd felt, she waited for him to respond.

"Bullshit. Who the fuck is this?" An image of her father and his flashing black eyes popped into her mind. Anger burned into her brain along with the pain of his invasion.

"*Stop it,*" she cried out, her hands reached blindly for the walls. She was a hybrid and didn't need blood on a regular basis, but the loss of her own blood was making her weak. From the new assault delivered into her head, she felt more of her precious life's blood pouring out of her nose and ears. Damn, maybe she shouldn't have shored up her walls so tightly.

"*Raina? It truly is you,*" he said, worry etched every syllable.

Strong arms wrapped around her. "Where do you think you are going, princess?"

She turned her head, meeting the black eyes of the monster she'd ran from, only now he was back to the devastating image of the man named Creed. "Please, just leave me alone. I want my mom," she whimpered.

"*Who is with you? Look at them. Let me see through your eyes.*"

"I can't. So tired." She tried to look at the man who now cradled her against his massive chest, marveling at the fact he wasn't covered in blood and gore. She wanted to do as her father demanded in her head, his voice rising until she was sure he'd pierce her eardrum, and she truly did want to obey. "Tell him I can't. Too tired."

Chapter Two

Creed held his woman, awed at the tiny thing in his arms. Her mumbled words made absolutely no sense to him. However, he knew he would protect her with his life. First order of business would be getting her the fuck out of Hell, and away from his bastard father. What the prick wanted with the sweet little thing that called to him, he had no clue, but she was his.

He navigated the tunnels, kicking the souls of the damned out of his way as he went. Their cries for help didn't faze him. The only reason they were in Hell to begin with had to mean they were the scum of the earth and deserved to be there. Some worse than others, some not as bad, but all deserved to be where they were. He wasn't their judge or jury, but he did consider himself the executioner in some cases. Luckily he was able to traverse to Earth, unlike his bastard father, thanks to his mother's blood running through his veins. Creed shook himself before he shifted to his demon form. He didn't want to scare his woman any more than she already was.

Damn, she was smaller than he'd pictured his mate being. However, she wasn't human. He inhaled trying to figure out what she was exactly, getting a hint of vampire and wolf. A smile lit his face. His mother would love his Chosen.

A rumble shook the entire cavern. In a burst of speed, Creed raced toward the entrance that would get him to Earth the fastest. The one place he knew they'd be safest. There, he'd find out why this woman was picked from the millions of others to be consort to the devil himself. The miles of twists and turns were filled with the pitiful beings who thought they could crawl out. He used his powers to keep them at bay, the scent of burning flesh so familiar he hated it. Another reason he and Satan didn't get along he presumed. While Creed was okay with killing those who deserved it, he didn't prey on the weak. Nor, did he spend much time in his father's realm.

The woman in his arms stirred, the smell of her apple and cinnamon scent mixed with the smell of her blood, had him hard as nails. "I'm a damn pervert to want an unconscious, bleeding, half-breed woman. What's the saying? Like father, like son?" He growled the question into the darkened tunnels.

"Are you talking to yourself?"

Creed nearly dropped his precious cargo at the whispered words. "Damn it, woman. You shouldn't scare a being like that," he said breathlessly.

He, the bastard son of the Devil himself was winded, and not from running. He could flash from one place to the next, but down here, he wasn't top dog. Not yet. Hopefully, not ever.

She tugged on his hair, the slight sting making him come to a stop. "Where are we going?" Her piercing blue eyes blinked up at him.

"I'm taking you to my home." He did his best to keep his eyes from turning red with need.

"I want to go to my home. My parents must be worried. My family are very important." Her body became rigid in his arms.

He wouldn't allow her to leave him until...well ever, but he wouldn't inform her of such things. Women, no matter what breed, tended to get all wigged out when they were told such things or so he was told. No, he'd hold that info back until he wooed her. Creed had never felt the need or urge to do such for any female until now. However, he had no doubt she would fall in line with him and his plans. Once he had some plans, other than escaping Hell that is.

The mental call the big bastard was sending out was grating on his ever last nerve, causing him to almost miss the invisible exit only a select few could access. Waving his hand around the perimeter, the usual glow that activated his signature didn't light up. "Mother of Light, give me the key," he muttered. With those words his access was accepted and he and his female were out the door, landing in the middle of a forest.

Creed glanced up at the glittering sky. "Looks like we ain't in Kansas anymore, princess."

"My brothers live in Kansas City. If you could just take me there."

If her words weren't said with such longing, he'd have laughed.

"Ah, baby, I promise you will love where we are going." His home was a veritable fortress where none of the bastard's minions could reach them. Of course, getting them there was going to take some doing, since he seemed to have been zapped with some sort of spell.

He rubbed his temple at the pounding that continued even though they were no longer within the realm of his father.

"You're bleeding." His woman said. That was when he realized he didn't know her name.

"What's your name, sweetness?"

Fingers that had been twisting in his hair, tugged without answering. "Listen here buddy, I appreciate you getting me out of that...dungeon, but you need to take me home. My father will be grateful, but if you continue to hold me against my will, you will be sorry."

He laughed, even though he knew it wasn't the smartest thing to do. Hell, many had said he'd been dropped on his head at birth. But hearing the beauty call *Hell* a dungeon was too damn funny. That was one mistake, the next was letting her slide out of his arms. He hadn't counted on the fact she was a supernatural being with powers, and damn it, he thought he could handle the tiny slip of a woman. When she shifted into her wolven form, he stared in awe at the beauty of her other form. Maybe he shouldn't have stared so long, then he wouldn't have missed the quick shift in her stance. Damn it, the woman, or now wolf, was faster and bigger than normal wolves.

Taking off after the wolf, he flashed in front of her. It took him a whole minute to catch up, and by then he wasn't sure who was more surprised by his appearance, her, or the being who appeared out of thin air. Creed quickly tackled the little wolf, then shifted her behind him, letting his demon form come to the front. "Leave now and you will live to see another day."

The blonde woman stood with the moon behind her, unfazed by Creed's words. "I don't believe I am all that skeered. Now, why don't you both play nice and follow me. Besides, I'm too tired to play fetch right now."

The scruff of the wolf in his palm turned into smooth skin as she shifted back. He didn't take his eyes off of the threat in front of him, realizing he was facing a female who may or may not be dangerous. "Listen, female, it would be in your best interest to turn around and walk away."

"She smells like my brothers," she whispered from behind.

Creed turned to see his woman dressed in the same clothing she had on looking paler than before. He caught her as she fainted.

Looking at the unblinking brown eyes of the sprite before him, then at the woman in his arms, he shook his head. "How is this so? Do I need to kill somebody?" Creed's mind reeled at the news.

The woman waved her hand. "You can try it, demon boy."

"I got your boy right here." Creed shifted his burden in one arm so he could grab his dick, emphasizing exactly what he meant. Mature? No, but he felt better. He called that a win.

"Do you kiss your mama with that mouth?" Blonde hair spilled to the side. "I should probably warn you that I'm keeping notes for all your infractions. That would probably be of some help for you to know. Now, let's start again."

"What is your name?" No way was he admitting he didn't know his own Chosen's name to this woman.

"My name is Jennaveve Grey, I am Fey, and you are in my realm. My friends call me Jenna, but for now, you may call me Jennaveve, while the little wolf may call me Jenna when she wakes. What are your names?"

"I am Creed." He thought it wise to answer since he didn't have a clue how to leave the realm he was in. His Chosen stared up at him, a small smile on her face.

"My name is Alecia Raina, but my friends call me Raina."

His body throbbed at the husky way she said her name. He let it flow through him, picturing it tattooed on his body.

Jenna snapped her fingers. "Hello, you still with me? Well, it looks like we have some things to discuss. Would you like to follow me to my home, or were you two just out for a lovely stroll through my property for shits and giggles?"

Looking up to the sky, he sighed. What the ever loving fuck? He asked his mother for a little help out of Hell, and she tosses him into this being's backyard. "Thanks, Mom."

"You talk to yourself often?" Dark brown eyes laughed at him from the Fey.

Creed had to fight the urge to toss a bolt through her chest. "Lead the way." He indicated the other woman should go first with a tilt of his chin.

Creed carried Raina for what seemed only minutes and then he was inside a large open area filled with books and a sitting area. When he'd said they weren't in Kansas, he truly had no idea where they were. Having dealt with the lowest of the low, instinctively he knew they could trust the Fey woman. The only question he had was where were they? And how the hell had they gotten there? Hell had many levels, which he'd traversed frequently. Being the son of Satan did have some privileges. The fact he was thousands of years old, there wasn't many things that shocked him, but being tossed into a realm filled with so much goodness was seriously fucking with his mind. Not that he was all bad. Creed had walked a fine line, leaning more on the side of good, only doing bad if you considered the ones he punished were the truly vile and evil. The lowest of the low.

Worry for Raina's well-being ate at him. She was too pale, and he didn't know if she could get the nourishment she needed in the realm they were in. His own blood was mixed with both his mother and father. The good and the worst. Not knowing how it would affect her, he didn't want to risk her safety. Once they got to his home, he'd get one of his employees on the task of procuring her a donor for feedings. Female of course.

"Your mind blocks are very good, Demon." The feminine voice came from next to him.

"Years of practice. You don't want just anyone wandering around in your head." The fact he'd been lost in his own musings and didn't realize she was so close, was a testament to his lack of control.

Jenna nodded. "How old do you think I am?"

For the first time, he looked at the being who'd changed into a purple maxi dress and sat across from him and Raina in a large pink chair like a queen, without an ounce of fear. At over six feet three or four he intimidated most everyone he met, especially with the amount of muscle he carried. He knew he was a very impressive sight for sure. Jenna, on the other hand, didn't look a day older than mid-twenties, and maybe a hundred and twenty pounds. At the outburst of giggles from the sprite, he narrowed his eyes. "You reading my mind again, Fey?"

"Truly, I look that young? That's totally awesome, but I am a few thou older than that I'm afraid. Like probably much older than you, I assure you." She wiped at her eyes.

"I don't want to play the 'I'm older than you game', but I'm up in the four number mark myself."

Jenna stopped and looked at Creed. "You're almost four hundred years old?"

Creed shook his head. "No. I'm over a thousand." He screwed his face up in a grimace. "Heck, I think I might be a couple, but honestly, I stopped counting. It upsets my mother."

She held her hand up. "Your name is Creed, which means faith. Who are your mother and father?"

Knowledge was power in their worlds. Black eyes flashed red and then back to black. "My father is the keeper of Hell, or the Devil himself. He has many names. Satan, Lucifer, Beelzebub, Dickhead. I could go on, but it could take a while. My mother is an angel who he seduced. She had me and shortly after I was born, gave me to him to raise." He gave a negligent shrug." I guess because I didn't quite look like a cherub, and wouldn't have been allowed to stay with her. They have shared custody if you will."

There was more to it, but Creed wasn't willing to go into the details of his twisted family. He let his eyes flash to red, knowing his skin would follow. The fact they'd landed in this being's realm must have a reason, and they were visitors. He would not be killing the woman on her home turf. Yet.

"Your father sounds like a lovely...oh, for fucksake, your father is an asshole. You know it, we all know it. However, he has his place. It's just not here." Jenna waved her hand around.

An undefinable expression flashed across her face. One that set off alarms in Creed's mind. He hadn't stayed alive as long as he had in Hell without listening to those warnings. He stood with Raina in his arms.

"Creed, you need to calm down." Raina spoke for the first time.

He glanced down, seeing his red skin against her paler one. "I'm sorry, Eros."

She smiled up at him even though he worried his other form would repulse her. No look of disgust or scent of fear came from her.

Raina rolled her eyes. "Silly man."

"You reading my mind?" He didn't feel her presence inside him.

"No, but your face is very expressive." Her hand traced his brow, soothing the beast within, then her eyes shut again.

"Come, I have had dinner prepared for you both." Jenna glided forward leaving them with nothing to do but follow. The comfortable room disappearing. A large estate that looked like a modern day castle appeared.

"You have a thing for kingdoms or what?" The sweet invitation grated on his nerves, making him want to lash out. He only wanted to take his Chosen home where he could ensure her safety, instead he was in some fairy land with a being he didn't completely trust.

"Be at ease, Demon. If I wanted to kill either of you, I would have already. Your mate needs blood, and I have no wish to see either of you harmed. I am still not sure how you came to my lands, but in the waiting area, you were approved for entrance. Otherwise you both would have been sent back to where you came from."

He reeled from her words. "Meaning we'd both have gone back to Hell? How secure is this place and exactly where are we?" Creed wanted answers, and his tone brooked no argument.

Jenna reached out and touched his arm. "Meaning you'd have gone back to your home, and she'd have gone to hers. I do no harm, unless provoked. Do not provoke me, Creed, Son of Satan." In that moment, he came to understand the façade the woman showed wasn't truly who she was. The laughing, joking woman hid a core of steel. They definitely had some things to work out, and it wasn't going to be easy. He wasn't used to taking orders, except from Satan, and that was only when he had to. Although Jenna may be older, and this was her home, Creed wasn't a boy, and he had a mate to protect.

He needed to make sure the home was secure. His own fortress was safe from his father and all his beings, but this place wasn't his.

The feel of wards blanketing the perimeter hit him the closer they got to the structure.

Without a doubt, there were several things Creed knew for a fact. One of them was that his father was going to want to kill him, the other...he would kill for his mate. Not that he blamed the other man. Hell, his father wanted to kill him on a daily basis as did most who met him. If they had the power to do so they'd try, but most lacked the skill or balls. However, this time Satan had a real reason. Creed had never truly done anything to warrant his father's wrath. Not like he'd done this day, taking his consort.

"Your wards will keep out most, but will they keep out my father and his demons?" The hairs on the back of his neck rose, a clear indication they were being watched. "You should tell your people to stand down. I don't want to hurt anyone."

Tilting her head to the side, Jenna seemed to be mulling over his words, then nodded. "Follow me."

He kept his laugh contained. "Absolutely. This is your home after all."

Jenna raised her middle finger, but didn't look back, making him laugh. Maybe they'd get along after all.

Raina stirred, her gorgeous dark eyes blinked open. "Where are we?"

He looked around the grand entryway, and had to admit it was pretty opulent. From the huge entrance with the white marble floor, to the double staircase on each side. He could imagine Christmas with garland and lights draped around the banisters, and a huge tree right in the middle. Why the hell he was getting all sentimental he had no clue, but immediately put the brakes on that train of thought. His home was just as magnificent although it was a bit darker. Halloween in human terms looked more appropriate in his home.

"Welcome to my home, Alecia Raina." Creed heard Jenna say but didn't acknowledge her words, waiting for Raina to say something. Anything. Finally, after minutes she blinked up at him, then looked at Jenna. Creed held his breath, unsure what he'd do if she demanded they take her to the home she'd lived in with her parents.

"You can put me down now." Her whispered words held more strength than before, but through the thin material he still felt the small shiver she tried to hide.

"You need nourishment, Mon Eros." His casual use of the word love made Raina blush, but that was exactly what she was to him. He could feel it in his very being. Already his heart was trying to reach out to hers. For hundreds of years he'd thought to die without ever knowing love, of ever finding the being meant for him. If his in-laws were hybrids, he'd figure out how to make it work...or else. The yawning years without her didn't appeal. Living in his father's world, knowing she was out there would be a death sentence to him. No. Creed would move any obstacle in order to make Raina love him.

"I've never needed blood the way full-bloods do." Raina looked at Jenna then the floor, her tone belied the fact she felt ashamed to admit the truth of her statement.

Creed allowed her legs to drop, keeping her face at eye level to his. "Do not feel guilty for a natural need, Eros. We all have certain things we need, yet I won't apologize for mine and neither should you. Everything about you is special and beautiful." He kept his eyes locked with Raina's.

She sucked in a deep breath, making her breasts brush against his chest. "When I have need, my father usually has a supply brought in. It's all very civilized."

He kept his thoughts to himself, but wished he could shake her father. Civilized and him had never been said in the same sentence. Well, unless you said he had just destroyed a civilization, but that was just semantics. "I can help you with the feeding, make you think it is like it was at your father's home, if you will allow me to," Creed offered.

"Hold up. We don't know how she'd react to your blood. I will provide proper nutrition here, and then we will see if you two are compatible." Jenna glanced between them.

Keeping his calm, Creed stared over Raina's shoulder. "I am aware of this. I'm also aware of the affects I have on vampires. This is not my first rodeo, Fey."

"Hey, be nice. She's just looking out for us." The heat that licked up his insides had nothing to do with the little fist she'd punched him with. Damn, he could just imagine her sucking him, and it wasn't his blood she was after.

Blue eyes that flashed to red squinted up at him. "You are thinking dirty thoughts aren't you?"

He tried to look innocent. "What makes you think that?"

Raina glanced down between them, then back up. "I'm pretty sure if I could see below our waists I'd be seeing you sporting a hard on. As it is, I'd wager my Mercedes on the fact you were totally picturing me sucking you, and not your neck."

Unable to stop himself, he laughed and hugged her tighter, letting her feel exactly how she affected him. Bringing her closer so he could whisper in her ear even though he knew the other woman would hear. "You would win that bet." Creed then licked the shell and nibbled on her lobe. The full body shiver it elicited made him groan as he could scent her arousal spike the very air.

"Hello, you are in the presence of others. Haven't you heard the saying about no PDA?" Jenna rolled her eyes.

Creed sighed and allowed her to stand on her own. "Stay beside me. If you feel threatened at all, call out to me." He touched his temple.

Her smile lit up his world. "I think I can handle myself, but thank you."

"Nothing will happen to her in my home. Geez, didn't I just say I saved you from like death or something. I mean I am like all powerful and stuff." Jenna threw her hands in the air and began walking away.

He really didn't want to argue with the woman. Especially not since they really did seem to owe her and he had no clue how to get to Earth, but the truth was, he had no clue if his father's minions could show up at any time. The last thought had him checking the wards protecting the Fey. If the scourge of the underworld came calling, he worried they would be like child's play if they had his father backing them. He hoped to create enough of a warning system they'd be able to escape if the worst did happen, although the Fey believed her realm was untouchable, in his experience, nothing was out of Satan's reach. Now that he found his Chosen, he would never put her at risk. The first sign of trouble, and he'd move Heaven and Earth to protect Raina.

Without moving a muscle, and from hundreds of years of knowledge, the extra wards needed to keep out even the Devil himself were in place without him having to think about it. He hoped.

Jenna sucked in a breath. "What did you do?"

"I have ensured all our safety. Even your friends. Now, we can all rest easily." He shrugged.

Chapter Three

Raina gripped Creed's hand. "Is that necessary?"

"What if one of my people tries to visit? Or someone tries to leave? Will they be killed on the spot?" Anger darkened her features.

Creed rolled his eyes. "You're being overly dramatic. I am not a young pup. My wards are like living, thinking extensions of me. When anyone gets too close, the wards reach out to me. If I'm busy then they make the decision to allow entry or not depending on the being."

"Jenna, if you don't want them up, then he will take them down." Raina jerked away from Creed, exasperation stamped on her beautiful features.

He could look at her face for an eternity and never tire. Porcelain skin with jet black hair that he'd swear had blue highlights under the overhead lighting. Her eyes reminded him of the bluest skies, drawing him in with promises of pleasure, but her air of innocence kept him in check. Instinctually he believed she wasn't as worldly as he. How would she feel about mating a demon? He'd sampled just about every creature known to man. Hell, he was thousands of years old. He looked at the tiny being the Fates had decided was his. Although he'd dallied in many sexual escapades, never had he found himself attracted to another man, and had never thought his mate would be a hybrid vampire/wolf shifter.

"Your wards may stay up. I have modified them for my people."

A quick check and he realized a pulsing vein of pure white light flowed throughout his wards.

Creed inclined his head. "Lead the way, my Lady. I do believe my Eros here is in need of some refreshment. I too could use a glass of your best hard liquor. Please tell me you have whiskey?"

"Of course. You should meet Kellen Stiles. I think that wolf has whiskey running though his veins." Jenna took the opportunity to reach for Raina's free hand, drawing her away from Creed for the first time. "You are scared?"

Her pulse jumped at Jenna's words, visible in the vein on the slim column of her throat. The clawing to have her back at his side eased at her words.

"Wouldn't you be?" She asked but didn't try to pull away.

Honestly, Creed would have been pissed if he'd been jerked from his home. But he kept that to himself. He followed, staying alert for signs of danger.

Inside the room they entered, Jenna waved at a couple who reminded him of pixies.

"This is Dane and Kandi. They helped to prepare you a meal and a suite for the evening. If you are going to be here longer, then they have also volunteered to help make sure you are both comfortable," Jenna said.

The male came forward with a short crystal glass and held it out to Creed, while the female had a taller glass for Raina.

Jenna took them both when Creed didn't. "Thank you, Kandi." She gave him a mock growl. He pulled Raina in with him. "You too, Dane."

"Sorry, Kandi and Dane. I forgot my manners." Creed winked at them both, taking the glasses from Jenna.

Dane's petite wife did a little curtsy, making him shake his head. Little Kandi would probably have a heart attack if she knew the Devils son, and a half vampire, half wolf shifter were standing in front of her.

Once the couple left, he sat, taking Raina with him. "Time for you to feed, Eros." Holding up the tall glass with the fresh lifesblood. "I can help you, or you can do it yourself. Either way you need this, your hunger pains me."

Raina licked her lips. "Thank you." With hands not quite steady she took the cup and drank her fill.

He took a sip, his own hunger pushed back until he was sure she was satisfied. The fact that he'd put another's needs first was a new thing for him. He glanced across the room and caught Jenna staring. In that moment, he realized she knew more than she was telling.

"Are you finished?" He asked when Raina sat back with a sigh.

"Yes. Now what?"

His body had an answer, but he was sure she was not up for that just yet. "Now, you need rest and we need to figure out just what the hell is going on."

"I need to contact my family or you will have an army falling down upon your home." Truth rang out in her quiet words.

Jenna crossed her arms. "I'm afraid that won't be possible. You see, only the Fey can contact here, and only the Fey can make contact out. I can be a go between if you want, and if you trust me."

Something in the other woman's eyes that belied her easy words, flashed.

"I'm afraid the wards will keep you from mentally contacting others and vice versa as well, Jenna. However, I should be able to reach out to my mother." Creed kept his eyes locked onto her pulse for any sign she was being dishonest.

"How do you reach your mother? A cellular device?" Jenna stared between him and Raina.

Raina laughed. Those gorgeous multifaceted eyes rolled before she gave a smile he'd love to see every day for eternity. "Of course we have cell phones. Well, I did until some snake thing took me away."

A snap of his fingers and a new phone was in his palm. "Here, this is yours. Whatever your old number was, just think it and it will be."

"Wow, you're powerful." She smiled.

"Oh, I love that phone. I have the same model. But, it still won't work here."

"Jenna, make it so."

Creed turned to see a dark haired beauty saunter into the room

"Talia, what did I say about staying out of this?"

The woman named Talia shrugged. "Yeah, well, you were torturing the poor girl who looks like she needs a hug from a motherly figure. Hence, I am here."

Before he knew what the other woman was going to do, she bent and hugged his mate. "All is well, child. Call your mama, and let her know you are safe and the big bad Fey Queen has her bitch pants in a twist, because her twin mates are assholes."

"Talia, Damian and Lucas are not assholes. They are just...male," Jenna cried.

Raina jumped up. "Did you just say Damian and Lucas? As in Damian and Lucas Cordell?"

Talia moved next to Raina. "Now Jenna, you know them boys are randy, so if they slept with this sweet thing it's not her fault."

Creed growled. He felt his horns grow and his skin stretch. A sure sign he was not in control, while his Chosen started laughing like a loon. And to make matters worse, the Fey queen looked ready to do real damage.

"Oh my gawd. This is awesome, except the part about me and you know... I have never. I mean ewwww. They are my brothers." Raina made some gagging noises. "Seriously, I just threw up in my mouth. That's why you smell like them. You're their mate? Where are they?" Raina looked around.

Talia fell into a chair, her laughter grating on his last nerve.

"So you're their baby sister? I thought her name was Alecia?" Jenna sat next to Talia and smacked the other woman in the arm as she continued to giggle.

"I go by Raina. Fate must have decided to send us here since we are connected. Where are my brothers?" She asked again.

Jenna took a deep breath. "You may call your parents now."

"I'm really nervous. What do I say to them?" Raina looked at him then Jenna.

Creed shrugged, figuring he had no experience to offer in such situations. The fact he had a past with the elder Cordells was something he needed to address. He looked at his Chosen and wondered how he should handle it...her. His mind raced with worry at how she'd react to the knowledge that he'd known her mother long before she'd been created.

"That's what I thought. I must warn you both...I'm sort of considered the baby, and as such, my family is a little overprotective." Chewing on her lower lip, Raina dialed a number.

"Alecia Raina Cordell, where the hell are you, girl?" A booming voice yelled through the line.

She winced. "Now, Daddy, don't freak out, but I was sort of dragged into Hell."

Creed's eyes widened as he felt power trying to break through his wards.

"Let me speak with your father, Eros." Creed held out his hand.

Damikan Cordell's low growl could be heard through the phone. A lesser man would have pissed himself.

Raina shook her head. "I don't think that is a good idea, Creed."

"Who is with you?" Her father spat the word.

He didn't let the Vampire Kings words shake him. He'd faced worse beings and lived to tell the tale. Now, he waited for his Chosen to hand the phone over.

"Be nice. Both of you," she admonished before placing the slim rose gold device into his large palm.

"I'm always nice." He brushed a kiss across her lips, the action making her gasp.

"Hello, Damikan. How are you and your lovely wife Luna?" The ache he'd felt anytime he'd thought he'd never have a mate of his own, no longer there. He glanced down at the beautiful creature before him, and realized for the first time what the Fates must have had in store for him. The reality of his situation had him chuckling into the phone.

"Listen you, bastard. If you touch one hair on her head, I will kill you slowly. I will make you wish for death, but not allow you that, until I alone deem it is time." The words were spoken in a low menacing voice. If Creed had been there, he was sure Damikan would have reduced him to ash.

Realizing he didn't want the conversation to be overheard, he put a shield around himself. "I would never do anything to harm my Chosen. Your daughter is the light to my dark. Without her, I would sooner die than continue on." He shook his head, trying to figure out a way to make Raina's father understand. "If I open myself to you, I am allowing you the opportunity to kill me. I don't do this lightly, but to show you my true feelings. I know you remember me as I you. Had I not saved your mate's life all those years ago, she'd not have lived to birth my true Chosen. Loneliness is a cold beast that makes a man hard. She brought sunshine into my dark life. Now, fate has brought me and Raina together. Had I not been there at the time I was, Luna would have been killed before you'd met her, hence keeping her from creating the being meant for me. I guess fate has a fucked up sense of humor." Creed glanced over to see the trio of women staring at him.

"You are right. I do not trust you. How do I know it is not a trap?" Damikan was wise to question everything he said.

"Because your daughter is in my care. If I wanted to hurt her, would I have allowed her to call you? Wouldn't I have just killed her, or sent little pieces of her body to you? That would have been more effective." A father's love for his child was nothing to mess with, especially for a vampire. Their offspring was few and far between. Only because Damikan bonded with a shifter had he produced not one, but three children. His oldest were twin boys Damian and Lucas. Adversaries that Creed admired.

Damikan sighed. "My mate says to allow you to show us. She is linked to me."

A grin tugged at his lips. Luna had a way of making the huge Vampire King bow down to her wishes. "Tell Luna I said hello, and I am sorry for the grief I have caused."

"All is forgiven. It has been hundreds of years. I don't carry grudges. Not like some people," Luna teased.

He could easily see her looking at her mate, the love would be apparent, and was happy to admit there were no ill feelings. "This I am glad to hear. Now, are you both ready to see inside my mind? I must warn you, I have had many adventures over the course of the past few centuries." The need to warn them seemed prudent.

Damikan laughed. "Believe me, there is nothing you can show me that I haven't seen, or done."

Yeah, everyone thought they were worldly, until they were faced with things they hadn't been challenged with. "Don't say I didn't caution you. Try to focus on the present instead of the past. It'll be less stressful for you, old man." Creed couldn't help the taunt. He allowed his shields to come down, knowing they'd see what they chose. The good, the bad, and the ugly.

"I can see why you thought my mate was yours." Damikan broke into his thoughts.

"How is she? How did she get into Hell and why?" Luna's voice shook on the last word.

"There is more, I just don't know if you are ready for it. Suffice to say, your daughter will be well taken care of." Creed brought the wall down for Raina and the others to hear the last of his conversation.

"Eros, your parents are reassured of your well-being. However, if they have need to speak with you they can." At least he hoped they were. There was nothing but silence from Damikan since he'd shown them his memories, other than acknowledgement of understanding. The Vampire King would have to understand, at least as a man, what it was like when one found his other half. He met the electric blue stare of his mate, and felt her tapping at his mind. Of course, a father would have a hard time accepting his baby girl growing up and all that would entail. He handed the phone to Raina and watched as she paced and spoke to her parents.

His mind sought Raina's as well. Her perfect porcelain skin and piercing blue eyes were such a contrast between his much darker ones. He knew she was one of the few who could walk in the sun thanks to her mother being a shifter. It was a closely guarded secret that the Cordells had worked hard to preserve, and one he had never in all his years ever thought to betray. Now, he was grateful his own Chosen could enjoy such things.

"My father would like to speak with you again." Raina held the phone out.

Creed rose with the grace of the predator he was. "This is Creed. How may I be of service to you?"

Damikan snorted. "So formal. You can start by explaining how you came to be in Hell." Even though he'd appeared the debonair man all those centuries ago, he still hadn't shown his true self. A fact he should have realized meant Luna wasn't meant for him.

"That is easy. It is where I grew up, and the home of my...shall we say, father, for lack of better terms. Although, I will say there is no love between the two of us."

Raina raised her head to the ceiling. Creed was being purposefully obtuse. To him Damikan was not his king.

Creed waited for the inevitable explosion, but he was not one to cower to anyone, least of all his Chosen's father. Start as you mean to go on has always been his motto, and the last way he meant to go on was licking the boots of a man who was probably younger than he. Oh, that didn't mean he wouldn't respect the man as the father of his woman, but he wouldn't allow the man to talk down to him. Hell, his own father ruled the entire underworld with an iron-spiked fist, and Creed didn't shake in fear when the bastard brought the hammer down on him. Repeatedly. Even if that meant he would have to regrow limbs lost. Not even if it took him years to heal. Nope, he was a stubborn bastard that way, in more ways than one.

"I don't think I like your tone, boy," Damikan said in a menacing tone.

He made sure the other being could see the image he projected. "I got your boy, boy," Creed said without heat.

Raina gasped. "Creed that is my father. You can't talk to him that way." She jumped up, reaching for the phone he easily held out of her reach.

"He started it." On her next jump, Creed grabbed her around the waist and held her against him.

"And what are you, a two year old?" She tried for the phone again.

He looked to Jenna for help, but the woman seemed more amused at the display than anything. "I do not remember being two. Two hundred, maybe. Two thousand, most assuredly."

The sound of the couple on the other end of the phone gasping had him stilling.

"Exactly how old are you?" Damikan asked in a measured voice.

"Do you really want to know? Be very sure before you answer, for once you have this knowledge, you can never...well actually, I can take it away. Although it is painful I'm told." Creed tossed the phone to Jenna as Raina's squirming was demanding more of his attention. "Deal with that. I don't need the phone to talk to them."

Jenna caught the phone in her hand and pressed a button. "Hello again."

"Is the man you are standing near able to hear us?" Damikan asked.

"Tell him the answer is yes." Creed walked over to a chair and settled down with Raina in his lap. She looked tired.

"Let me have that phone back, please," Raina pleaded

"Raina, honey, are you safe?" Luna's voice came over the speaker loud and clear, holding a note of fear Creed had never heard his own mother display.

"Luna, I can assure you, your daughter has never been safer than she is right this instant. Whatever took her was able to do so under you and your family's nose. I'm not accusing, I'm just stating fact. Until the threat is stabilized or eliminated, the best place for her is with Creed."

"What is this Creed to her?" Damikan asked the million dollar question.

"She is his Chosen, I believe that is the term he uses. You would call it in your world a Hearts Love. No matter the name, she is his other half that much is true. Fate has decided for them, and for better or worse, we will work together to keep her safe."

"Daddy, my wolf recognized him from the very beginning." She looked at him.

"I want my baby girl home. Why don't you bring her here where we can protect her with my Elite soldiers?" The demanding King was back.

Creed shook his head, a chuckle escaped. "Sir, I believe we are where my father can't reach us, other than Heaven, there are not many places he doesn't have access. I can block all our paths from my father, but if his minions come to you, they will be able to extract information from anyone in your household. And before you say you are too strong, remember you are dealing with the ruler of the Underworld. If you'd been here, he could get that info, and possibly send someone here."

He let his words sink in and waited. Raina's eyes widened. When she didn't immediately jump up and demand he let her go, his heart resumed its usual beat.

"Jenna, explain to him what my Elite and I are capable of. Yes, she may have been taken from my home, but that was a mistake that will never be repeated. I foolishly thought nobody would dare trespass. Believe me, I've corrected that oversite," he growled, every bit as fiercely as any wolf.

"Be that as it may, I won't allow her safety to be tested. You don't know him like I do. He won't stop, unless I stop him." Creed wrapped his arms around Raina. The thought of her back in the waiting room outside his father's court sent a cold chill down his spine. Never!

"Mom, tell your husband that he needs to accept his baby girl is grown." Raina rolled her eyes. "Listen, I'm tired and really want to rest. I'll call you both in twenty-four hours. Every twenty-four hours, okay?" She looked to him for confirmation.

He nodded, and watched as Jenna gave her assent as well. At least they were on the same page.

"If you don't call me every twenty-four hours on the dot, I will track you down, and there will be Hell on Earth to pay. Do you hear me Creed and Jenna of the Fey?" Damikan threatened.

Creed smiled, while Jenna didn't look the least bit fazed.

"And, Jenna. I do believe there are two very anxious young men looking for you. The last time I saw you we had taken you back to my home." Censure clear in the words had Jenna turning away from them.

"I apologize for disappearing on you and your wife, but I needed my realm to heal properly."

"Don't let him upset you, dear. However, have you tried reaching out to Damien or Lucas?" Luna asked.

Jenna and Talia stood. "I need to rest. I am not at a hundred percent still." With a regal nod, she folded her hands.

"Got it, old man. Now, off to bed with you folks." Creed waited till Raina said her goodbyes, then disconnected the call, making sure there was no link back to them.

"Now what." Raina asked.

Jenna took a deep breath. "Now, we rest."

Jenna and Talia both stood. The two women looking exact opposites. Talia tall and dark while Jenna was petite and blonde. He smelled wolf and fey mixed with Talia's blood, while Jenna's was the purest of white light he'd ever experienced. Jenna reminded him of his mother.

The Fey glanced over her shoulder, a knowing smirk on her lips. "Come, I'll show you to your rooms."

"Rooms? Don't you mean our room?" Raina gripped Creed's hand tighter.

Creed's blood heated. "You sure, Eros?"

She nodded. "I'm not saying I'm ready to make love, I just don't want to be alone in a strange place."

He licked his lips, then sucked in air as she stood on her toes and initiated a kiss. For all of a second he allowed her to lead, then he palmed the back of her head and took control. His tongue traced the top of her mouth, then tangled with hers. Minutes, or hours could have passed, then he was letting her move back.

"Holy fuck," Creed whispered.

"No humping in the hall. It's a rule."

Dazed blue eyes rimmed with red blinked at him. "You are totally lethal."

"You ain't seen nothing yet," he assured her.

Chapter Four

Raina wasn't sure what she'd expected, but kissing Creed was even better than she'd imagined. In all her dreams of the future, she'd pictured her mate, but never had he been the actual son of the Devil. Sure, she'd imagined a bad boy, but Creed was the ultimate one.

The room they entered was purple and gold with splashes of red in accents. Raina smiled at the whimsical room. A huge bed dominated the space with a dresser and full length mirror on one wall, while a small sitting area sat off to the side. If she had to describe what the inside of a genie's lantern would look like, the space she stood in would be exactly what she'd expect.

"I'm glad you approve. There is a full ensuite through that door." Jenna pointed toward an arched doorway. "If you need anything just pick up the phone next to the bed, it'll ring Kandi or Dane."

Creed turned and murmured something she didn't catch, then shut the door.

"This is amazing. I mean seriously. It's like a fairytale." Raina spun in a circle, her arms spread wide.

He crossed the space separating them after closing the door, power flowing around her letting her know he'd ensured their safety. In two long strides he was next to her, crowding her. "You want to shower, or would you like me to take care of your needs?"

His hands cupped her face as his words registered. "I can take care of myself."

"Yes, I am aware," he said, then those full, sensual lips of his moved down, and Raina forgot what he'd asked.

She wanted to sink into him and not think about anything or anyone but the two of them. For the first time in her life she wasn't the pampered princess, youngest child of the Vampire King. She was a woman who was wanted by a man for herself. Giving herself over, she allowed the feel of having his lips on hers be the only thing to register.

The kiss turned into more the minute his tongue traced her lips. His warm body and strong arms controlled every nuance. Now as his tongue licked along hers, a thrill went through her unlike anything she'd ever experienced. His masterful way he controlled her with one hand on the nape of her neck, sent an added layer of need through her.

"Oh, Goddess. What are you doing to me?" Her entire body lit up like she had electricity going through her from a conduit.

His hands on her hips roamed up and down, holding her tightly to him. "Needing you. Letting you feel what you do to me."

She pressed against him, and longed to have more intimacy, but wanted to know more about him. "Can you hold me? Talk to me?"

When his mouth came down on hers, she was prepared for more of his heated kisses. However, the sweet ones were just as devastating. "Don't ever doubt I can't give you what you need, Mon Eros. You ask and I will move mountains for you."

There was no doubt in her mind that he meant every word he said. "I'd do the same for you."

His hunger was evident in the hard erection pressing against her stomach, and the fast beat of his heart. Although he stroked his huge hands over her from hips, to breasts, to ass, and made sure she felt him rubbing against her front, he didn't seem to mind her calling a halt.

"Thank you for saving me, Creed." She wrapped her arms around his neck.

He kissed her jaw, then licked her lobe. "If you were reading my mind, you'd see exactly the things I'm imagining doing to you."

Standing on her tiptoes, she nipped his chin. "Open your mind and let me see. I bet you'd be shocked if you read mine as well, dirty boy." A shiver worked through her as she realized she'd never been so outrageous in her entire life, let alone with a virtual stranger.

"I'm not a stranger," he whispered.

His low growl made her start as she realized he'd read her mind. "*You can hear me?*"

"*Yes, and you can hear me, too. You can also see inside me.*" The sexy tone in her head sounded the same as when he talked outside.

She worried her lower lip, then he spun her to face the bed. "Climb into bed."

Her clothes disappeared, leaving her in a comfortable sleepshirt that looked more like a man's button down. "Thank you."

His warm breath feathered over her neck. "I'll look forward to having you naked. Until then, I enjoy having something of mine on your body, that way when I strip you, and kiss every delectable inch of you from your lips to your toes and back, you'll remember me."

"I'll always remember every moment with you." A yawn caught her by surprise.

"Let's sleep, and then we will get to know one another better tomorrow." He lifted her onto the bed. "Make no mistake though, we will be bonded for life."

With him leaning over her, she should feel small, yet she didn't. "I want that, too. In all my life I've planned what I'd do when I found my Hearts Love. Trust me when I say you are exactly as I imagined him to be."

The bed dipped from his weight climbing over her. "When I have you stripped bare for me, I'll touch every bit of your soft flesh with my fingers, then I'll trace the same path with my lips. I'm going to play with your body until you are begging me to take you, then I'll join our bodies. My heart is already reaching for yours."

The low words made her brain fog with lust. She could smell her own arousal and wondered if he could as well.

He slipped off her. "Fuck, you smell delicious." A masculine groan filled the air.

Almost forgetting her plan to wait, she rolled to the side propping herself on her hand. "You're too gorgeous for words, Creed. Tomorrow is another day." Her hand traced his ripped abs.

"Don't be shocked if you wake to me humping the air," he joked.

Laughing she fell forward, resting her head on his chest. "I am pretty sure you will not need to resort to such measures. I should warn you about something," she paused unsure how he'd react to what she said next. "I sometimes dream walk. It's not intentional, and only when I'm extremely tired."

A stiffness invaded his limbs. He gripped her by the back of the hair, forcing her head up to meet his eyes. "Have you ever done so with someone you didn't know? Ever dreamt where you saw something you shouldn't?"

Raina thought about his questions before answering. "Not to my knowledge, no."

He relaxed, then petted her head while his breathing evened out. "My father may have sensed you that way though. Dream walkers are coveted in Hell because if they can be twisted, they can do a lot of damage to a person's psyche if they are properly trained, and believe me, Satan trains his pets well."

His body was warm beneath hers, which was an unusual thing for her since she'd never slept with another man before in all her years. The even strum of his heart and blood flowing through his veins lulled her into a light doze. She didn't know what to think of the past twenty-four hours and if what Creed said was true, then she had a lot to think and worry about. His father was Satan for Goddess sake. A huge part of her worried how they'd get past that obstacle, the other part, the most feminine part, wanted to claim him in the way of her kind. He called her his Chosen, but what did that mean to him? For her people, they bonded for life. No divorce, no other. Ever.

Taking a few measured breaths, she let sleep come to her. Even when she slept, she was able to control where she went. In the dream world, nothing was foreign to her.

Only the world she found herself in was far different than any she'd seen before. She turned in a slow circle taking in the strange place. The sky above looked like nothing she'd ever seen before. The fact there was no sun or moon worried her. Even the Fey world had a gorgeous sky. Here the view above was an eerie red and black with varying shades of orange.

She wrapped her arms around her middle as a warm heat whipped around her, her mind spinning. Off in the distance a huge structure that looked straight out of Grimm's Fairy Tales stood with flying creatures circling the towers. Acting on instinct she took a step back, stopping when her foot sunk into something soft. "Holy shit," she swore as she stared at what looked like a lake of lava spread out as far as the eye could see behind her. Mountains of black hills were beyond that. Pushing the fear back, Raina reached for the control she'd always had in the dream world. The man's shirt was replaced with black leather leggings and a black leather top that fit her like a glove, covering her completely from neck to ankles. She hummed, her body moving forward on autopilot. A look down at her hands showed they were trembling slightly, and her heart was threatening to pound out of her chest. For the first time, she was truly scared. Which pissed her off more than she liked to admit.

Her mind reached for Creed. He had to be near. This world must be where he was from. Images of their flight from the chamber he'd rushed them from looked nothing like this, but the farther she walked, the more she understood this was his home.

"What are we doing here?"

The deep growl had her spinning. "I followed you." She answered. Wariness filled his gaze, slowly being replaced with something undefinable.

He came closer. "This is my father, or should I say Satan's home. He will know we are here."

She opened her mouth to disagree, the very fact she could control dreams usually meant nobody else could interrupt them. "Why would he need a dream walker?"

"You can enter others dreams, right?" At her nod he continued. "He must want you for something specific. Or, he wants to see if he can breed a dream walker with you. If he can get a child mixed with his blood and a dream walker, the combination could be...deadly."

"I'd never do anything for him willingly." She ran her hands up his hard pecs, feeling them flex under her palms.

He deliberately let his gaze drop to her mouth. "Ah, sweet Raina. My father is far from the cajoling type. He would use anyone, or anything to make you do what he wanted. Imagine him having control of someone you love above all others. If he was to threaten their very existence, would you do anything to protect them? Even go into someone's dream and manipulate it?"

She opened her mouth to deny his words, then snapped it shut as he put his hand up.

"I know you, Raina. And sadly, my father knows you, too. He makes it his business to find out these things." He looked off toward the towering structure in the distance.

Her mind opened to his completely. In the waking world she'd feared allowing him complete access to her being, yet now, with his soul laid bare, she wanted to give him the same. Years of torment at his father's hands assaulted her. She wanted to cry at the image of the little boy he'd been, wanting to be loved by the one man who should have loved him unconditionally, only to be kicked away like a dog. The years flashed by and she could see how he'd become a fighter for those who were wrongfully accused on Earth. Her heart swelled with love for Creed. Her wolf snarled at the many women who came and went in his life. It hadn't occurred to her he'd have so many, although she should have realized since he was thousands of years old. Her wolf growled while the vampire half of her had her fangs dropping.

The red and black world disappeared, replaced by the purple room they'd been given. She blinked down at Creed. His eyes opened, love shining up at her.

"Can I just say that all those women were just practice for when I met you?" His words came out gruffly.

Little bit by little bit, the anger faded. The past was in the past. The future was yet to be decided. The present was a gift she was definitely going to open with both hands.

"I think we should leave all that locked into a box at the back of both our minds." She knew her cheeks were probably a deep shade of pink, and was glad for the fact they were in the dark.

He pushed up and rolled them over. "I would do anything to erase all the others from my mind, and my history. Anything to never see you hurt, Mon Eros." She opened her mouth, but he placed his finger over it. "I'm not done yet. You don't understand the loneliness I have felt for thousands of years. When I felt a tug on my heart, it was as if my soul was being pulled out of my body. I had to go to that chamber. Seeing you there, I would have gladly killed any being who hurt you. So yes, I have done things in my past I'm not proud of, but if you give me half a chance, I swear to be the best man you could ever want. Hell, I'll even be nice to your father and brothers."

She stared at him for a moment, then leaned up and kissed him, hard, then deliberately pulled back. "That is the sweetest thing anyone has ever said to me. Make love to me, Creed."

Creed couldn't believe his ears. He'd never been at a loss for words, yet hearing her ask him to love her, to make love to her, he found he was beyond stunned. All he thought about for years was to one day find the one woman who would love him unconditionally. Never did he actually think she'd exist, especially one as gorgeous and good as Raina. Her soul called to him, like they'd been connected long before she'd been created. The Fates had a profound way of making things work, and in this one, he owed them. His entire life up till this moment had been nothing.

He realized he was nervous as he stared at her. Her arousal called to him the longer he lay looking down at her. "I love you, Raina."

"And I you, Creed. I'm not an experienced woman like you're used to." He silenced her with a scorching kiss, one he felt all the way to his marrow.

She moaned, licking at his tongue. He tilted his head, his own mouth and tongue wanting to dominate even though he knew her wolf wanted control, when he nicked his tongue on something sharp. The metallic scent of his blood made him hiss. He looked down to see her blue eyes turn red. The vampire half of her sucked on his injury, seeming to enjoy his taste.

He pulled back, not giving her too much of his essence out of worry for what his lifesblood would do to her. "Easy, Eros. We don't know what my blood will do to you."

She pouted up at him. "Both my sides want to bond with you. In order to do that I'll need to bite you."

He knelt above her, his body rock hard at wanting just that. To feel her fangs sinking deep within him. He knew his own eyes had probably turned red. A glance at his forearms resting next to her head, he could see they were red as well. Yeah, he waited to see how she'd react to the demon half of him.

"How big do you get in your other form?" She ran her hand up his bicep.

A shiver wracked him at the lack of disgust in her voice. "Depends if I'm in a battle, or just angry. Most times, if I just shift, I am about seven and a half. However, I think closer to eight if in battle. Of course, I haven't actually measured."

She licked her bottom lip. "Are we done talking now?"

"You still want to be with me," he asked gruffly.

"More than anything. I'll try to keep my fangs to myself," she said with an impish grin.

He laughed. "One day you can sink them into me, anywhere, anytime."

Her deep inhale made her breasts brush against his chest.

Time for talking past.

"You smell so good, Creed. Even when I first saw you, I wanted to lick you." Raina's arms came up and pulled his head down. She nuzzled his neck, growling as she did, making his spine tingle.

"Fuck, that is sexy as hell. I scented you as well. I would have ripped the arms off of anyone who dared touch you. Now, how about this shirt disappearing?" He sat back on his heels, thinking of using his powers, then discarding the notion. One by one, he popped the buttons open. Her creamy flesh appeared even smoother next to his, making him aware of their differences. With effort, he pushed his demon side back. The need to be careful so as not to hurt her beat at him.

"You can't hurt me." She echoed his thoughts.

"Are you reading me?" He asked, opening the last button on the shirt.

There was a moment of hesitation before she answered. "I think we are still connected. Can't you see what I think and feel?"

He stopped and looked inside her mind. Wonder filled him as he realized she'd been open all this time, while he'd been more concerned with what she'd think of his long life and past. His brief pause clearly caused her to worry what he read in her memories, and he rushed to reassure. "Mon Eros, I want you now like none other. I don't know if I'm worthy. No, scratch that. I know I'm not, but I'm not noble enough to let you go. If you want out, say so now, and you'll have a fighting chance to be free." He released the ends of his shirt, holding his hands out to the side. "Make the decision quickly though, because once I make love to you, I will never let you go. Bond or not. You are mine. Do you understand?"

She chewed her bottom lip. "Creed, do you understand that there is only one Hearts Love for my people?"

He raised his brows and waited.

"What that means is, you are it for me, silly man." She pressed her tiny hand over his heart, making it skip a beat, then speed up. "There is no turning back, unless you don't want me. In here, what do you feel? Do you not feel the same? Don't ask me to go, please." Tears shimmered in her eyes.

It was his turn to growl. "Never. I'm never letting you go. I clearly didn't do a good job of letting you know how much you mean to me with words. How about I show you instead."

"Normally, I'd say words are better, but by all means." She nodded.

With a chuckle, he laced their fingers together and moved back over her body. "You are too precious for words."

His kind also claimed their mates by marking them, combining their essence by exchanging fluids with a bite. It took supreme effort for him to make his other half understand they would claim Raina soon. She was their Chosen, regardless if they could never claim her fully.

"Look at me," he ordered.

Once she made eye contact, he bent and kissed her. Then releasing her hands, he slowly slid one hand down her stomach while she wrapped her arms around his neck. Their tongues slid together in a dance of their own while his fingers found her wet and warm. He parted her legs with his own, then delved his hand between her thighs. She canted her hips in welcome, making him chuckle. He rubbed her clit before stroking farther down to her pussy, pushing inside. With each pass he gathered more of her cream and spread it over her clit, sweeping and circling it then going back to her entrance and doing it again. She trembled the faster he moved his fingers, while he never stayed long at either place, prolonging her pleasure.

She gripped his hair, pulling her mouth away from his. "Please, Creed."

"Please what, Eros?" He licked her neck, flicking his nail against her clit faster. "Do you want me to do that?"

"Oh, yes. Yes that." She tilted her hips up.

"Or do you want me to fuck you with my fingers." He pushed two digits deep, then added a third. She was so tight, her inner walls squeezing him.

"That, too. Everything."

Pushing his fingers inside her, he rubbed his palm against her clit and worked her to a hard fast orgasm. It was all he could do to keep from sinking his teeth into her exposed flesh as she wrapped her strong arms around him and pulled him to her.

She shuddered, moaning as the mini contractions still shook her and he continued to work his fingers in and out of her.

Her arousal coated his fingers when he pulled them out. He sat back and licked, taking her flavor into his mouth.

"I need to be in you. Are you sure?" If she said no, he would surely go insane, but he'd pull back.

"More sure than anything else in my life. Make me yours." She reached between them, running her hand up and down his cock, her thumb brushed over the tip.

He shuddered, untangling her fingers from his cock, then dropped forward, spreading her thighs farther apart. Looking down, he swore he'd never seen anything sexier in his entire life.

Anxious to join with her, he grasped his cock with one hand, ran the tip along her wetness coating it with her cream, then pushed inside. A harsh groan at how hot she was escaped his throat before he could stop it. Pulling back then pushing forward, he slowly entered her until he was seated all the way to his balls.

"Damn, you are like a searing inferno gripping me like a wet hot glove. Don't move or I'll come like a boy on his first time." He settled into the V of her hips, holding completely still.

She panted. "I don't think I can move. You're huge. Like did you grow a third leg or what?"

He suppressed a chuckle. "You're good for my ego." After a few moments, he felt her relax. Drawing himself out, he then surged forward. In and out, he set up a pace ensured to satisfy them both. Wanting to prolong both their pleasures, he eased one hand beneath her hips, angling her up slightly, he made sure his pelvis hit her clit on each downward thrust. The action making her cry out sharply. He felt her pussy clench down on him, making him plunge back in and out faster, losing his rhythm for a second.

She began thrusting against him, her moans driving him wild. The idea he could hold back his own impending orgasm became laughable. Needing her to go with him, he reached between their bodies, flicking his finger over her hardened little clit. The bundle of nerves already primed and ready only took a few swipes of his ministrations, and then she was screaming his name in ecstasy. He groaned loudly, joining her as his own climax shook him to his very core. The loud roar shocked him, thick black claws near her head had him jerking back in horror as they ripped into the bedding. His demon wanted his mate.

Raina gasped and panted beneath him, red glowing eyes stared up at him, breath sawing out of her. "My demon," she growled.

His claws retracted, the demon settling back inside pleased she'd accepted a part of him. Falling onto his elbows, he rested his forehead against hers. "I'm sorry I lost control."

Her smile was like the sun coming out on a cloudy day. "That was wonderful. Don't apologize for what we did. I love you and your demon form. Does my wolf repulse you?"

He rolled to his side, taking her with him, his cock still inside her. "Goddess no. Why would you ask that?"

"Because it's different than you are. I'm different than you. Isn't that why you thought I'd despise your other side?" she whispered in a rough voice, cuddling against him.

Her eyes were closed but he could see inside her, feel her real worry he'd not love every facet of her being. His own insecurity had caused her to second guess his feelings, and for that he wanted to kick his own ass. There wasn't any other woman, or being in all the realms he would want for his Chosen. He let her see in his heart how he felt.

"I am sorry, Raina. If I could take back the past few minutes and erase the hurt I caused you I would. Trust and believe you are the perfect Chosen for me. Hell, too perfect for me, but I will spend the rest of eternity making sure you know how much I love you, and do the best I can to be a good mate to you and our children if we are blessed to have them." The thought of her bearing his young had his dick jerking inside her.

"Well, I think that idea has made you very excited," she laughed.

"Are you not too sore?" He gave her a suspicious look, no way was he willing to hurt her for his own selfish pleasures.

"She snorted, lifting to straddle him. "I'm half wolf, half vampire. I have awesome healing powers. Now, I just need a little lesson on what to do." She rocked back and forth.

"Ah, I think you are doing just fine." He groaned as she began swiveling her hips. Creed's eyes crossed and then he couldn't think as she began moving up and down. His hands gripped her ass, helping her move faster.

He was thousands of years old, had more women than he cared to remember, yet the tiny woman who claimed his heart, mind, and soul brought him to an orgasm with her in no time. They both came together, shouting each other's name so loudly he figured if the Fey hadn't soundproofed the room they were in, then the entire castle surely overheard them.

Chapter Five

Creed stretched, wondering what had disturbed his sleep. A presence in the room he didn't recognize, but one he knew wasn't a threat, had him throwing back the cover. Not wanting to disturb his Chosen, he made sure she continued to sleep with a whisper into her mind. He waved his hand over the bed, invisible shields formed a dome, the protection spell one he and he alone, would be able to breach. With a thought he donned a pair of slacks.

"What brings you here, Alpha?" Creed asked by way of greeting. The wolf's scent was clear to him. Although he wasn't Raina's alpha, the fact the tattooed man before him was in charge of a pack was clear in his aura.

"My name is Kellen Stiles. Sorry to interrupt you so early, and most def in your bedroom. Jenna has a bit of explaining to do on that account," he growled, looking toward the closed door.

He was glad to see the other man wasn't comfortable at the fact he'd popped into what was essentially Creed and Raina's bedroom. "I'm sure you are aware my name is Creed, and the gorgeous creature sleeping is my Chosen Raina."

Kellen inclined his head. "I'm aware of both your names thanks to Jenna." He took a deep breath. "You'll have to excuse me. Fuck, this shit makes me nauseous." Kellen ran his right hand over his head, the rings covering his hand catching Creed's eyes.

"Why don't you skip the pleasantries and just get right to the nuts and bolts of your visit. I'm assuming this isn't a social call. I'm also assuming you don't visit the Fey world much either if the unhealthy hue to your skin tone is anything to go by." Creed towered over the alpha, but he sensed no fear from him. Interesting since he usually made others quake just by standing next to them.

A grin quirked the corner of Kellen's lips. "I like your thinking. Alright, I'm gonna lay this out for you. That little lady's brothers are a pain in my motherfucking ass. I need you to return to Earth so they will get the fuck out of my club before I rip their throats out. Because if I do that, then my mate will be pissed. If my mate is pissed, then I don't get laid. When I don't get laid then my pack faces my ire. Hence the shit rolls down. Feel me?"

"Basically, this is all about you getting laid?" Creed nodded knowingly.

Kellen raised his brow. "Pretty much. Plus, if I killed those two, Jenna would be hurt. I sort of like the little Fey. Don't tell her I said that."

He tried to wrap his mind around what the hell that meant, but the covers rustling had him glancing back toward the bed. "My Chosen and I didn't come here voluntarily, you understand?"

"How did you get here?" Kellen didn't look over to the bed.

Creed's respect for the alpha went up tenfold. "I'm assuming you know who and what I am?"

"I didn't ask questions, although I know you are not wolf, nor are you vampire or human."

He tilted his head, wondering what the alpha would do or say once he realized he was talking to the son of Satan and an Angel mixed. The words were out of his mouth before he could call them back.

"Damn, boy. That is quite the combo." Kellen rubbed thumb over his bottom lip. "So, you take after your dad or mom?"

Unable to help himself, Creed laughed. "Do you want to know if I collect souls for the good, or the bad side?"

"No. I mean do you have wings like an angel, or horns like a devil. I mean wings would be cool, except they'd get in the way. Horns, they would sort of give you away unless you could hide them and shit."

The seriousness in his voice and expression wasn't lost on Creed. He searched the alpha's face and mind, coming up against a wall that kept him from seeing inside him. However, being as old as he was, he was pretty good at reading others, and came to a decision. "I have wings, and I can transport from place to place as long as I know where I want to go, or if I can lock onto a person. As for horns...I have them in my demon form. So, I guess the answer is, I take more after daddy dearest in that way. Although, I am not a soul collector. Now," he growled.

"What does that mean?" Kellen's hands went to his hips, the tattoos on his arms jerked as his muscles flexed.

"Meaning I'm not a boy, Kellen. As a matter of fact, I have seen worlds come and go for thousands of years. So yes, I've collected the damned for my father, but only those who were truly evil and vile. I've never once in all my time been one of my father's minions. He has plenty who do that for him."

"Good to know. Alright then. You bringing her back or what? I don't want to be killing the Cordell twins, but I'm this close." He held his thumb and pointer finger together.

Creed laughed. He liked the man and his one track mind. "Why doesn't Jenna bring them here? The reason we are here is to keep Raina out of the way of my father."

Kellen shrugged. "Probably cause they get on her nerves. Hell, they get on mine, and I wouldn't have to be sandwiched between them. Yeah, I just threw up in my mouth on that one."

Shaking his head, Creed looked toward the bed to see if Raina still slept. His mind reached out to her. He hoped she wasn't dream walking, especially when he wasn't there to monitor where she went. If his father wanted to capture her, he'd try it when she was most vulnerable.

"I'm going to go persuade one Fey to put two Wolpires out of their misery." Kellen strode toward the door.

"Wolpires?" Creed asked, walking with him.

At the door, Kellen looked over his shoulder and shrugged. "The mix of wolf and vampires. Seems a fitting name."

The door clicked shut behind him, Kellen's voice sounding muffled as he yelled for Jenna. Creed snorted out a laugh. The big bad alpha had a demented sense of humor, or he was just plain crazy. Either way, Creed was glad he was gone. Staring down at his woman's sleeping form, he marveled at the miracle he was given.

"I'll protect you with every fiber of my being, and beyond." He made the vow, knowing he'd die to protect her.

Raina heard Creed and another man speaking. She tried to pry her eyes open, but something kept her from waking completely. A sinister presence like a black fog surrounded her, pulling her deeper into slumber.

She looked around the unfamiliar setting. Darkness intruded, making her breath catch in her throat. She swallowed against the fear. Never had she been unable to manipulate the dream world. Pulling on her experience, she harnessed control. Light appeared all around, showing her where she was. "Dang, maybe it was better when I couldn't see."

Back in the valley where she'd been during her dream walk with Creed, only now she stared at the castle that was closer than before. The barren ground under her feet crunched all around her as beings went about their business, paying no mind to her. Heat buffeted her legs, scorching in its intensity. In that moment clarity hit her that she wore only the shirt of Creed's. Her thoughts skittered as she tried to manifest thick leather clothing to protect her from head to toe. When the action took more effort than normal, she was breathing hard as the last article covered her flesh. Pulling her hair back, she secured it with a band from her wrist, not wanting to expand any more energy than necessary by using her mind. Whatever was going on in the dream was draining her.

A loud hiss to her right had her jerking around, claws extended. The sight of a small childlike creature siting on a large boulder eating what looked like the remains of an arm, revolted her.

"You don't belong here," it hissed.

Raina shook her head. "Why are you here?"

The thing licked its treat, then tossed it onto a pile of other bones. "I live here." It waved a boney arm in an arc. "You smell like bastard."

Raina's back straightened. "Excuse me?"

The thing leapt through the air like a spider monkey before Raina could anticipate its move, landing on her back. "My brother, the bastard. You smell like him." It inhaled deeply. "Where is he?"

She nearly cried out as the thing jerked her head back at an angle sure to decapitate a human. Unwilling to be the next victim to the creature, Raina reached over her shoulder and jerked the creature off, tossing her away with her enhanced strength. "If you plan to hurt Creed, you'll have to go through me." Her wolf pushed to the surface partially, mixing with her vampire. She allowed the thing now crouched and ready to attack to see the long claws and fangs she sported. Her eyes would be the red of her vampire, and if needed, she'd morph into her wolf to rip whatever she faced to shreds.

"You dare threaten me on his behalf?" The creature sat back on its ass. "You like my Creed?"

Hearing the thing in front of her refer to Creed as hers had a shard of jealousy ripping through her. True, the man was thousands of years old, and she'd known he'd had many lovers of all species, but looking at the tiny creature that looked more childlike than female...Raina couldn't wrap her mind around the idea.

"Oh, stop looking at me like that, sicko. Creed's like my brother. In fact, he's my Halfling. We share the same father, sort of. Although Satan doesn't claim me the way he does Creed. Not that I care you understand," it hissed.

The ground rumbled before Raina could ask more, making the creature scramble back to its boulder. "Come, you must not be down there."

She stared at the outstretched hand with the long bony fingers that had only moments ago been holding a human arm. Looking at the piles of skeletons, Raina hesitated.

"They were all pedophiles." The disgust evident in its voice held no trace of subterfuge.

"I really need to shore up my walls," Raina muttered.

"What is your name, thing of Creed's?"

Raina leapt onto the top of the boulder instead of taking the hand offered. "Raina. What is yours?" She stood, and looked around.

As the ground below stopped shifting, red lava poured out of where she had been, melting the very spot.

"Does that happen often?" Her eyes took in the scene, then looked at the little thing crouched next to her.

"Kyrene is I. I am female like you." She tilted her head to the side. "That happens when he is mad." Her finger pointed toward the castle.

Fucking great! She knew for a fact if you died in the dream world, then you died in the real one. Usually she was the one in control, but she was not the one with the power this time. Her only hope lay at the hands of the being who was bent on claiming her. Hell would freeze over before she allowed him to lay one finger on her, or those she loved.

"Oh I've seen that look before. It is usually just before heads rolled," Kyrene muttered. "Where is Creed?"

"I wish I knew." Raina inhaled deeply. "Do you know how to leave this realm?"

When Kyrene nearly fell off the rock with her wheezing laughter, Raina almost gave her the extra push. Her humanity and the reminder this was Creed's relation stayed her action.

"Nobody leaves. This is the Master's world. You can check out anytime you like." She waved at the pile of bones. "Lots of ways to do that. But, there is no way to leave the way you are suggesting, unless you are Creed, or one of His minions." Kyrene shuddered.

"How did you get here?" Raina wanted Creed. She wanted to wake up. Dammit, she felt like crying.

Kyrene scooted forward, then stood. At five foot five inches Raina was considered average height, and she had thought the crouched thing...no female would be small. Yet as she stood, they were almost eye-to-eye. In a blink, Kyrene shifted into a lovely looking woman. "Don't look so shocked, Raina who smells of Creed. We all have facades. You think my mother wasn't smart enough to ensure I knew how to protect myself from harm, before she was no longer of use?"

Raina held her ground as Kyrene began walking around her. The rhythmic swaying of the other beings' body almost hypnotic. In her world of paranormal knowledge, she should have known not to trust anyone at face value. The childlike image, and the use of Creed's name had lured her in. Well, if this thing thought she'd be an easy kill, she had another think coming.

"I guess you surprised me. What with the crouching child, hidden beauty routine. Raina let her wolf push forward just enough her bones were ready should she need the extra power.

"I'm not sure what you are referencing, but I feel it has something to do with your culture." Kyrene stopped in front of her. "Tell me something. What would you do to save your own life? Would you give up something precious, like Creed, or your first born child?"

The thought of giving up either of the things Kyrene suggested would be worse than death. "Never," she said with vehemence, her words came out a deep growl as her wolf agreed.

"Hmm, interesting." Kyrene reached out to touch the side of Raina's face.

Tired of watching the swaying form, and fear of the unknown had her shoving her arm into the chest of the creature in front of her. Red eyes widened before a smile flitted across Kyrene's face. The demon fell off the boulder, leaving Raina alone to watch as she fell onto the red ground.

"You pack a hard punch, youngling." Kyrene sat with her legs crossed, lava flowing all around her, the red liquid moving past her without touching.

"I think you have been underestimated." The words again came out with the stress on the s.

She'd seen her father and brothers shift to half wolf, half vampire enough times, and if she'd ever needed to tap into that ability, now was the time. If this thing was related to Creed, sparing her would be something that she'd try to do, but only if the creature didn't do anything stupid.

Her claws came out, fangs dropped. The sound of seams ripping was loud to her ears. "You want to see how much you underestimated me, bitch. Bring it," she said, waving her fingers, which didn't look anything like a humans any longer. She braced for impact, knowing even in her altered form she'd not be able to take the heat from the melting ground.

Beady red eyes narrowed, then Kyrene was crouching. "You don't want to fight with me, thing of Creed."

Shaking her head, Raina agreed. "I don't want to fight anyone. However, I will gut you and see what color you bleed."

Creed looked back at the bed, expecting to see Raina where he'd left her. His feet froze at the sight that met his eyes. An empty bed, and the smell of brimstone. "Motherfucker," he yelled.

The foundation shook beneath him, his demon form took over. Their mate was gone, and they wanted blood.

"Calm down, Creed."

He turned toward the door, staring at the tiny Fey. "I need to go back to Hell. They have Raina."

Kellen tried to put his body between him and the female. "You need to chill, dude."

Looking at the alpha, he tried to figure out what the hell he was seeing. "What are you?"

"Hello, you really asking me that." Kellen looked Creed up and down, then sighed.

"You know what, I don't give a flying fuck what you are. Fey, I need out of here. Raina is gone."

Jenna stepped closer to the bed with Kellen right next to her. In the next instant, the air seemed to suck out of the room. Two men Creed had never laid eyes on entered the room, their bodies vibrated with anger, yet he scented Raina on them. Instantly, he wanted their heads on a platter.

"Where is she?" He reached them in a few strides, holding each up off the floor by their neck.

Voices rang in his ears, but all he wanted to hear was where his Chosen was. His black claws pricked their skin making blood well. His nose twitched as he inhaled the familiar scent.

"Why do you smell like my Raina?" His red skin was startling next to their tan all-American looking ones. "Speak now, or forever lose your ability to do so."

The fact they were identical all of a sudden registered. They were blond, while his Raina was dark as night. He brought them closer to him, inhaling deeply.

"If he fucking tries to kiss me, I'm gutting him." Brown eyes blinked out of a face that most women probably thought was handsome.

"Shut up, Damien. No need to piss off Big Red here. Now, listen, unless you want my big brother to get really angry, you should probably let us go so we can work together to find our sister."

The one named Damien smirked. "Baby bro is trying to be nice. I am finding I am not wanting to bleed all over our Hearts Love's home."

Jenna gasped. "Boys, really. Let's not do this in front of company."

"Little Fey, we are as far from boys as this thing is from a human. Now, release us, before I get a real good mad on. My baby sister would not be happy if we gelded you."

"Will you two wear a fucking sticker with your names on it for fucksake? Yo, big red dude, you're wasting time trying to kill those two. They are not the enemies. Well, I mean, they would kill for your woman. Now, I did want to kill them, but that's another story." Kellen's deep voice came from beside him.

Creed allowed the two beings feet to touch the ground. "You got here, you can get out. How?" He asked, not stepping away or releasing them completely.

"We were finally able to track her here. Shit, she's gone." Damien moved his hands in the air, electricity crackled.

"You don't want to go where she is. Just get me there, and I will bring her home safely," Creed swore.

At the exact same time, Damien and Lucas disappeared. He spun, expecting them to come at him. Only they stood next to the petite Fey. Their focus completely on her.

"You, little love, are in so much trouble once we get back from rescuing our sister. Now, before you add more infractions onto the laundry list we've already compiled, I suggest you zip it." Damien covered her lips with his, followed by Lucas.

Creed wasn't one to judge. "If you two are done sucking face, could you please get me the fuck out of here?" The last word was yelled so loud even his own ears hurt.

"We will all go," Kellen said.

"You all will die. No, scratch that. In order to go to my world, you must be dead. Nobody goes to Hell who is alive. Are you all fucking nuts?" He clenched his fists.

Jenna held her fingers against her lips. "They might be a little, but I do think you need a little backup, and in my mind, you are going to need them."

One of the twins looked down at her. "You trying to get rid of us?"

Her eyes widened in shock and horror at his words. Creed was an expert at reading those two emotions, having seen them his entire existence.

"How many is that now, Lucas?"

"I believe the Iron Wolves call it a shitton." The man's eyes shifted to red.

Damien shook his head. "Nah, I think we moved right on to the fuckton I heard them talk about." His eyes too had gone from brown to red.

The Fey stepped from between them, her arms going out to her sides. "You two are the dumbest, most gorgeous mates. You are lucky I am too weak to zap both your asses." Her fingers moved as if she was reaching for her powers. The scent of her tears hit him, and if she were his, he'd be begging for forgiveness.

"While I do appreciate this soap opera, I need to be going. Every moment we fuck off here, is a moment she is in my father's clutches. Do you know what he had planned for her?" He shot the images of what he had seen done to those his father chose to be his consort. The willing, and the not, into both Cordell twins minds. The last thing he expected was the alpha of the Iron Wolves to shift into the beast he'd partially seen and attack him.

Although Creed was still over eight feet in his demon form, the wolf with his iron looking claws came at him without fear.

The vicious, dirty assault had a whole new appreciation flowing through Creed. He deflected the first swipe of the deadly looking claws, getting sliced with the next. He stilled as Kellen came at him again, coming low in what was sure to separate his intestines from him. Creed had fought many opponents, but never had he met one whose arms and legs moved as fast as this ones. His own claws met the flesh, yet he found himself unable to truly make a killing blow.

"Enough," Jenna screamed. Her arms out, long blonde hair flowing around her.

Wind buffeted him, pushing him away from Kellen. They both fought an unseen force, trying to get at each other.

"Kellen Stiles, I said enough. Do you want me to send you back to Laikyn with a pink bow in your hair? I will totally do that, and you will even have matching nails. Try me, boy." Her eyes swirled, no longer the same brown, but the palest blue he's ever seen.

"Be easy, Fey Queen. I will not hurt him. I just want to go to my Chosen." Creed pulled his demon back, returning to his natural looking state.

Kellen snorted. "Yeah, you keep thinking that, demon." He raised his hands at Jenna's shriek.

Even the Cordell twins appeared apprehensive of their woman.

"Baby, you need to dial it back before you hurt yourself."

She turned to the speaker. "Shut it, Lucas."

The speaker who must be Lucas made a show of his thumb and pointer finger running across his lips.

"Can you get us to the Hell realm if Dumb and Dumber can get a lock on their sister again?" She pointed over her shoulder.

Creed nodded. "Absofuckinglutely."

"You are not going with us. Period." Damien glared at Jenna.

"In that we are in agreement." Kellen cracked his knuckles.

"I will have to agree with them. And, before you say anything, you have too much light in you. Once you entered Hell with us, Satan would know and the jig would be up. If we have a chance of saving my Chosen, we will need to use a little stealth."

Jenna took a deep breath. "Fine, but I expect all of you to come back safely."

"See, I told you she cared."

"Lucas, I swear by all that I love I will kick your ass one day." Damien took a step closer to Jenna.

Creed turned away, giving them a sense of privacy. His eyes caught Kellen's. "So, what the fuck are you exactly?"

Kellen shook his head. "I'm the Iron Wolf. What the fuck are you, the original Hell Boy?"

He thought of grabbing his dick and telling him he had his boy, but shook his head. "I'm not quite a demon, yet not an angel." He left it at that.

"Cool. I think my mate Laikyn would say the same about me. You'll have to come to my club and have a drink. Do you drink whiskey, or what?"

"Does a bear shit in the woods?"

"I think we'll get along just fine." Kellen held out his hand.

Looking at the tattooed arm and the man willing to go into the depths of Hell with him, Creed took the outstretched hand.

"Awe, look. A bromance happening right before our eyes, Damien."

"Can I kill them?" Creed tilted his head toward the twins.

Kellen sighed, the sound truly regretful. "Sadly, I've asked the same thing, and been told no each time."

Chapter Six

Raina knew they were being watched. Clearly Kyrene realized it at the same time as well. Her body shifted back to the form she'd been in when Raina first saw her.

"Come, we must hide," she hissed, waving her hand, impatience stamped on the childlike face.

She looked around them, trying to figure out which one of the damned was responsible for the threat she could feel coming.

"Thing of Creed. I implore you to come with me. I will not let any harm come to you. This I swear on my life."

A glimpse of Creed and the creature playing together entered her mind before Raina could shore up her walls.

"Raina. My name is Raina, not thing of Creed's." She hopped down from her place and stepped carefully over the charred remains. Her boots sinking into the softened ground.

"Hurry, they are coming." Kyrene ran, her hand grabbing Raina's.

Without looking back, she could feel they were being stalked. Where they could hide, she had no clue. Heck, she didn't know if this creature was leading her to the Devil himself. Like a lamb to the slaughter was a thought that blinked like neon lights in her mind, but she ignored it.

They practically flew across the ground, their feet leaving little indents in the black ash for anyone to follow. *I'm not a hunter, and even I could track us.* She expended a little energy, wiping away their tracks.

"What did you do?" Kyrene questioned at a rocky cliff.

She looked back, air sawing in and out of her. No way up, and down looked like a black abyss straight out of a horror movie with fog shrouding her vision. Taking a step back, she tried to move away. Kyrene's grip tightened. "We must go down. It is the only way."

"Fuck that. Hell is down." Her heart threatened to beat out of her damn chest.

"No, Hell was straight ahead. Actually, it's all around you. Down here, is my home. Sanctuary if you will. Come, I promise it's not as scary as you think. Climb on my back."

Raina laughed. She couldn't help it. This childlike spider monkey creature wanted her to climb onto her back, and descend further into the depths of Hell. Sure, and sign her up for a waterfront property while she was at it please. Not!

"How do I know you aren't taking me straight to him? Or luring me into a trap? Or just going to kill me?" Proud of herself for speaking in complete sentences, she waited for answers.

The last thing she'd expected was Kyrene to morph into the lovely woman and take her choices away from her. "I tried it the nice way," she muttered, then she gripped Raina around the waist and jumped over the edge.

A terrified squeal escaped Raina as they fell, or rather as they jumped off the craggy edge into the pitch black. Wind whipped past, the heat hotter the farther they fell. She forgot to adjust her inner temperature. Forgot she could see in the dark. In all honesty, she almost forgot to breathe. Panic had her gripping Kyrene around the waist in a death grip that would have killed a human.

"You're fucking insane." Raina squeaked out before a bony hand covered her mouth.

The Johnny Cash song about falling into a burning ring of fire began playing through her mind the farther they fell, and she was sure any second she'd go up in flames. At the last moment, her two halves must have taken control and her body cooled of its own accord, for she had no recollection of doing it.

They landed on a surprisingly cool grey ground. Kyrene gave her a hug, then stepped back. "You are very dramatic." Sighing she paced away. "Poor Creed, getting stuck with a thing as drama ridden as he himself is. I'm not sure this era is prepared for two of you. What if you procreate?" She spun around. "Are you with spawn?"

Raina put her hand out as Kyrene looked ready to touch her stomach. "Come near me again, thing of whatever, and I will gut you from head to ass. We clear?"

Kyrene tossed her hands in the air. "That's the thanks I get for saving your skinny hide? Do you have any idea what those Gallo demons would have done had they found you? Let me tell you so you don't stress that little brain of yours. They'd have first fought over who got the head. That being *your* head. They enjoy brains you see. Then, they'd have had a free for all, splitting you between them. Or should I say whoever was strong enough to rip bits of you away from the others. Oh, did I mention they don't care that Satan has claimed you as his next whore. They are mindless things that search for their next meal, and you would have been a nice feast."

"How about you? Why won't they eat you?" Raina ran a hand over her arms, the imagery of the scene had gooseflesh popping up.

She laughed, the sound held no mirth. "They have tried."

The childlike image disappeared again, replaced by the woman. Raina wanted to know which her true form was, and which the façade was. "Where are we?" She asked instead.

"Home," Kyrene said walking toward a cave.

With nothing else to do but follow, she surveyed the area. Her vampire half ached, while her wolf scented predators close. Down here, neither half felt like they were the top of the food chain.

At the cave entrance Kyrene stopped and chanted. The words too low for even Raina's enhanced hearing to pick up, then a veil seemed to lift.

"Come quickly, thing of Creed's."

She bit her lip to keep from snapping and followed. Once inside, her eyes took a moment to adjust to the light. The saying Creed had muttered about being in Kansas popped out, making Kyrene smile.

"Not what you expected? I may be a demon, but I do like my creature comforts. Make yourself comfortable." The demon disappeared behind a sliding door.

Low comfortable looking chairs in hues of blues and pale pinks were so at odds with what she'd expected, Raina was still standing when Kyrene returned.

"I am sure you are hungry, but I don't think my blood is good for your kind. I also can't get you any. The best thing to do is wait for Creed. He will come for you." She flopped onto a huge chair, one that swallowed her small frame and looked as if she used it a lot.

"How do you know he'll come for me?" Taking the seat across from Creed's sister she waited.

Kyrene smiled, her teeth looked human. "Palease. You are here. He will come. The question is how did you get here? Which, I happen to know the answer to. Why haven't you asked that one?"

"Alright, I'll bite. How did I get here, and how do you know the answer to that?" If she was the one who brought her here to lure Creed back, Raina would kill her, and to hell with the consequences.

"Ah, I can see the wheels turning in your head. Yes, I did facilitate your return. You see, I too am a dream walker like you. I didn't know you were my Halfling's Chosen when I snatched you from your dreams. Ole Satan Dearest left that out, the bastard. I was to take you straight to him, but something had me stopping for a chitchat with you first, luckily for you." She flicked a piece of lint off her shirt.

Raina unclenched her jaw. "So, you are his what...errand girl? You do as Daddy says?"

Kyrene's eyes flashed to red. "Watch your mouth or I'll send you to him without a backwards glance."

Standing, Raina glared down at the other woman. "Go ahead and try it." She allowed her body to partially shift, readying for battle. No way in all the realms would she go without a fight.

"Fuckidy duck, I hate being good. It's so much better to just snatch and kill. But no, I have to grow one of those conscious things," she mumbled.

"You mean a conscience?" Raina watched as Kyrene began pacing, prepared to battle if the need arose.

Nodding, the demon waved her hand. "Whatever the word is I don't like it. Creed has been a very bad influence on me. My mother said he would be the death of me."

Creed had been in and out of Hell for thousands of years, but usually of his own volition. The only time he'd needed help leaving was the last time, and never had he tried to enter without alerting anyone. He was the bastard son, feared by just about everyone, and with good cause. Now, he was taking in three beings who were so far removed from ones who should be there, most likely on a deadly mission, yet he truly gave less than no fucks. Yeah, he was a bastard. The only thing he cared about was finding Raina, and securing her safety. He'd then do his damnedest to ensure the men with him made it out alive, if not a little worse for wear. He owed them at least that much.

"Alright, men. Don't talk to the locals. Don't eat the locals. Don't let the locals eat you. Any questions?" Creed asked once their feet hit solid ground.

Lucas raised his hand, but Kellen placed his palm over his face. "Shut it, or so help me I will not be responsible if only one of you are able to make babies in the future."

The man placed his hand over his dick. "I thought we were friends."

Kellen shrugged. "I haven't killed you yet."

Damien looked up at the black sky. "Why?"

Fed up, Creed began walking. "Try to keep up and shut up for the love of all."

Through his bond, he searched for traces of Raina. Damning the fact they were unable to exchange essences out of fear of what his blood would do to her. His mind reached for hers.

Frustration ate at him. "Can either of you reach her?"

"Let me try?" Damien's eyes swirled with power, flashing to red.

Lucas jerked next to him, his body the exact replica of Damien's. "What the hell is a Gallo demon?"

"She is with a being named Kyrene but she isn't sure if she is friend or foe. They escaped the Gallo, but said they were searching for them."

Creed growled, the sound one he was sure the beasts around them would know what it meant. His demon, unhappy their Chosen had been threatened, pushed forward, skin stretching, uncaring that his woman's brothers would see his other form completely. "Follow me. If you can't keep up, you will die. She is with my Halfling who may or may not die by my hand. No one is to touch her but me." Knowing exactly how he sounded and appeared to them, he walked away before he saw the fear, or revulsion in their eyes.

"Dude, our brother-in-law is fucking awesome."

"Lucas, you really need to turn your stupid meter down." Kellen's voice sounded exasperated.

He held his hand up. Several things became evident. One, was the brothers were funny as shit, and he would probably like them after he got over the urge to kill them. Two, Kellen was a deadly adversary and he was glad the wolf was on his side. Three, they were surrounded by Gallo demons. "Guys, I hate to break it to you, but we are surrounded by at least ten of some of the nastiest demons on this level of Hell. Now, I don't have to tell you how to fight I'm hoping, but just for shits and giggles, don't get dead, and don't let them rip your head off. They enjoy the brains first."

"Lucas is in the clear." Damien dodged his brothers' fist, then each man became focused on the fight.

The first wave hit, streams of creatures he was sure none of the men with him had thought to ever see. Creed took out two, his claws ripping their stomachs open, then taking off their heads in two swipes each.

Kellen watched, then did the same with one who attacked him. Creed spun, looking for his next victim. The Cordell twins fought like two extensions of the same being. His distraction allowed a horde of smaller Gallo demons to launch themselves at him. The pain of their teeth sinking into his arms and legs had him yelling in both agony, and anger. Razor sharp teeth ripped into his flesh, tearing into him while sucking on his lifesblood. He growled, knocking the ones on his arms off, then slicing the heads off the two on his legs. Luckily, their poisoned saliva didn't affect him, yet he stumbled as he tossed another Gallo away. They were like cockroaches, breeding without a worry for population control.

"Die you fucking prick," Kellen growled lobbing a head in the air, then made a show of hitting it with his fist like a baseball.

"He shoots, he scores," Lucas called out.

Creed watched as the trio used a Gallo demon as a bat, knocking into another. The blood and other matter flying everywhere. He shook his head, arms flying out to the side as he felt two more trying to sneak up on him and kick out as one jumped. The sound of crunching bones, and tearing flesh went on for another ten minutes. Ten minutes which allowed his rage to build as he thought of what Raina could be going through. In all his thousands of years, he'd never felt nearly as much as he did at that moment. The need to decimate everyone and everything that stood between him and his woman flooded him. Power raced through his veins like the hottest place in Hell he'd ever been.

"Ah, shit. Someone has unleashed the power."

He turned to see who'd spoken, the beings behind him looking smaller than before.

Kellen raised his arms. "We're on your side, big guy. Let's go find Raina. Remember, your Chosen?"

He stepped on the remains of a Gallo, then over a rock, the scent of Raina all over the area. "This way," he growled.

At the edge of the cliff he stopped. "You coming or what?"

"Dude, you wanna slow your roll. We ain't twelve feet tall like you." Kellen stopped next to him.

Creed pointed down. "We go down."

"Can we like hitch a ride with you?" asked Damien. Creed looked at the speaker, was sure it was the older of the two.

He grabbed the three men, then stepped off the edge. The fact none of the men squealed like little girls got them some brownie points. Landing on the edge of his Halfling's cave, the ground fell apart, making him scramble forward with his three burdens.

"Motherfuckinghellsomebitch," Kellen cursed, rolling to his feet.

"Like I said, nobody kills my Halfling."

Lucas looked a little green, but stood straight. "Let's do that again, like never."

His brother slapped him on the back. "Buck up. It could've been worse. We could've kept falling, or got eaten."

"What's the plan? We stand out here and yell till someone comes and lets us in, or something else tries to kill us?" Kellen's words echoed around them.

Creed ignored them, walking up to the wall, pounding his fist with a singular purpose. "Kyrene, open the fuck up or I'll tear this entire mountain apart."

He raised his fist prepared to do just that as the veil lifted. Kyrene stood with her ash blonde hair all around her in drab grey clothes, soot covering her, from head to toe. She looked frail, but he knew she was anything but. "Where is she, Halfling?"

"I've missed you, too. Oh, and I am great. Thanks so much for asking."

The scent of his Chosen's fear hit him. Without missing a beat, he lifted Kyrene, sat her down behind him and entered the home. "Raina," he breathed.

"Creed, how are you here?" She was up and in his arms.

"So, yeah, we are with Big Red. I'm Lucas, and this is my brother Damien. As long as you haven't hurt our sister Raina, we won't hurt you."

"How have you survived without strangling them all these years?" Creed lifted Raina into his arms, cradling her like the precious thing that she was.

"Probably the same way you haven't Kyrene."

He looked back at their siblings and Kellen standing with their arms crossed, glaring at him. "Point taken."

"Now that we are all here, I guess father-deadliest will be here shortly," Kyrene said with a grin.

Not liking the look on the younger demon's face, he placed Raina on her feet. "We need to get Raina and you out of here. If Satan finds you here." His words were cut off as a creature scuttled into the cave, his eye darting wildly about.

"KyKy, he's coming. Run," he gasped.

Kyrene flicked her hand, knocking the creature back out the way he'd come.

"You set this up? You brought my Chosen here to lure me. Why?" Creed allowed his demon to come forward, knowing the battle with his father would be brutal, and deadly for him. His only hope was to get Raina, her family, and friend back to their realm.

"It's a matter of living, and living well. You think I enjoy scraping by on the pieces of shit I'm given? You think I want to be alone for the rest of my life?" She pounded her fist onto her chest. "I will be given a place at his side. I will be his favorite, instead of another forgotten bastard thrown away. I proved I could bring him your woman, and you. No longer will I be the bottom of the food chain, having to fight off Gallo demons every time I step foot outside these walls, or the thousands of other creatures who'd love nothing better than to have me for their snack."

Creed watched the façade of the beautiful creature he'd seen her put on, fade into the skeletal being he knew her to be. The hate demon of her mother's people completely taking over her appearance. Yes, he'd tried to visit her as often as he could, bringing her treats, and pretty things, all in the hopes it would fill her with light, but clearly it had failed. Her cave was supposed to be a safe place, not a prison, or somewhere she felt isolated.

He ran a hand down his face. "I don't know what he promised you, but you should know it's a lie. Satan doesn't keep his promises, and he sure as shit doesn't care about you, or any of his bastards. Kyrene, I cared for you. I saved you when nobody else would have."

"That was just another mistake in your long list, Creed, bastard son of an angel." The booming voice had him tensing.

Kyrene's home only had the one entrance, but Satan didn't need a door. He made his own, appearing behind Kyrene, his appearance a deeper shade of red than his own.

"Hello, Father. How's it going?" Creed smiled, showing no fear.

The Cordell twins looked ready to attack, but he pushed a singular thought into their minds, knowing the invasion would hurt them, yet it would be the only thing that would save them.

"Do not move or think about trying to hurt him. He will kill you without a thought and you'll never see your Jenna again."

"Wow, I never thought I'd see the day you'd control two alphas with ease. I'm impressed." He eased his arm around Kyrene's shoulders, the huge red forearm bulging with muscles looked even larger next to the hate demon. "Now, for this one, wasn't she good at getting your Chosen here?" A long, razor sharp nail raked down her jaw, black blood welled on Kyrene's cheek.

"Let her go. She did what you wanted," Creed gritted out.

Satan laughed. "Always the protector."

"You said I would be by your side," Kyrene tried to twist away.

"Foolish of you to believe me. You've served your purpose, and I have no more need of you"

Before Creed could reach the duo, Satan's talon grew. With their eyes locked, Satan took Kyrene's life, uncaring he'd killed his own flesh and blood.

Creed's roar of *no* shook the cave, yet he couldn't allow his focus to stray from protecting Raina. His father was devious, and if he so much as took a step away from his Chosen, Satan would take the opportunity to do his worst to her.

"What's the matter, boy, she was just a demon. I have hundreds of others just like her. Just like you. What I need is from that one." He pointed a finger at Raina. "I'll make a deal with you. After she gives me a son, I'll let you have what is left of her."

Twin growls came from behind him and he knew it was taking all of their strength not to attack, but the Cordells were doing as he'd instructed. Kellen was a mystery to him. The Iron Wolves alpha had been strangely quiet, yet he knew he'd be ready to strike if needed. What they all needed to know was this was one place they were all the lower men on the totem pole.

"I'm gonna have to regretfully decline your oh so generous offer. You see, she is my Chosen. That supersedes your crazy plan. How about you go find your own Chosen?" Creed placed Raina slightly behind him, focusing his inner light as he searched for the link to his mother. If anyone could get Raina and her people out of Hell, it was her.

The laugh grated on his nerves, but he held the black stare.

"You were one of the smarter of the bastards. Now, I tire of this. Give me the girl." His arm lifted and a thousand blades shot out of thin air.

Chapter Seven

Creed waved his arm, making the weapons disappear like nothing. "Stop playing, old man."

Satan clapped his hand, then they were no longer in the small cave, but his castle. "Ah, this is much better. I was getting claustrophobic in that small place. Not to mention there was a mess to clean up."

The mention of Kyrene was meant to hurt Creed, the barb hitting its mark, yet he pushed it to the corner of his mind to deal with later. "As you said, there are too many of us. Need to cull the weak."

"They don't belong here. Let them go, and I'll be your willing beating boy...again." Creed kept his eyes on Satan, watching as he took his seat on the black throne. He shook his head as he watched the bastard sit and casually drape one leg over an arm, while he rested his arm on one side, cradling his head in a palm.

Raina flinched, her fingers fisting into the material of his shirt. "No Creed," she whispered.

"Don't speak out loud. You must let me handle this, or you will suffer a fate worse than death. I have a plan." Sure it wasn't solid, nor good, but it was one that would see to their safety and removal.

"Why don't you put on a little show for me? It's been a while since I was truly...impressed." Satan's booming voice had a sardonic tone to it.

Turning to face Raina, he met the eyes of her brothers and Kellen. "Hold her and no matter what happens, do not interrupt or let her go."

All three men nodded, but none said a word. He bent with the intention of kissing his Chosen, then thought better of it. "*If I kiss you in front of him, it will give him a perverse pleasure. Know that I am doing so and remember.*"

A shield was put up between the four of them and the rest of the chamber, one he hastily constructed. "Let's do this."

"Very well. Let's make a deal, shall we?" Satan's horns grew, gleaming onyx that looked deadly, and were if he struck you with them. Only you wouldn't die, you'd be his, consumed into his body as an extension of him. He didn't take many into himself, only those he wanted, and Creed's soul was one he wanted. Part angel and a part of himself. The caveat, he couldn't kill his own son, however if Creed was killed of his own free will, then all bets were off.

A small horde of demons entered from all sides. The first wave as Creed liked to call them. He glanced at his Chosen and the men holding her, knowing they'd see him at his worst, and hoped they wouldn't hate what they saw. Although, he probably wouldn't survive. Most assuredly, he wouldn't, but he needed to buy time for his mother to get through the wards keeping her out. Once she did, she would know to get those four out. His mind was brought back to the battle as a giant claw raked across his back, and a fist rocked his front, he allowed more of his demon and angel to blend.

Black wings tipped in white sprung from his back. He manipulated them, making each tip a weapon as he spun, razor sharp feathers sliced, sending appendages flying. First wave gone, he looked down to see a few gashes had made their mark on his own flesh.

His wings retracted and he didn't have time to wait for the next attack. Females poured out, their gruesome forms went from distorted to the most gorgeous. Bodies covered in nothing but rotting flesh, became naked, voluptuous. A man's living fantasy come true. His demon roared at their touch, a blast of power sent them flying away.

"Quit playing, old man. You and I both know I would never betray my Chosen. Nor would I hurt a female of worth. Those are your slags." His father would stick his cock in anything with a hole.

Black eyes filled with rage glared at him. "Very well, let's skip to the finale, shall we."

Shit! His father's pets entered. Worse than the Gallo, yet very similar. These creatures looked like a mix of Satan and a goat. It's where the myth of Krampus came from. Fucker that he was could enter children's dreams and cause havoc on Christmas. They weren't limited in Hell though. Their hooved feet and goat like legs allowed them to leap great distances, while they could strike their prey with their hooves, and kill with one lash.

Smoke came from their snouts, hatred burned from their beady black eyes. Why couldn't any of them have an ounce of intelligence? "Could you not spawn anything with brains, Father?"

He lobbed the accusation, then prepared for battle, or did what he could to prepare. The Krampus demons didn't come at him one-on-one, but as a pack. They circled, showing they did indeed have some sort of brain. Some launched over his head, their hooves hitting his horns, bits of bone chipping off. If he unleashed his wings, they'd take no time in ripping them to shreds, as he'd experienced in the past. He'd have to cull the herd as their number was too great. Summoning two swords, he sliced through the head of one, then another, taking more kicks and hits. The pain making him stumble. He blocked out Raina's fear and worry, although he could scent her need to help, her overwhelming pain at seeing his lifesblood pouring from dozens of cuts.

Finally, when the Krampus were down to a manageable, somewhat, level, Creed let the deadly wings appear. A grin on Satan's lips let him know it was a tactical error he should have known the bastard had been waiting on. He'd been tired, and weakened from the battle and blood loss, but he should have known better.

Spinning to face the new threat, he was somewhat shocked to find more of the Krampus and Gallo demons, working their way toward him. The demons working together was a first, which meant his father really wanted him dead.

"Mother, I really need you to get my Chosen and her people out of here." He pushed out, knowing he wasn't going to survive. He'd lived thousands of years, now was as good a time as any to finally end it. He'd go down in a blaze of fucking glory, but not in front of Raina.

"I see it's gonna take an army to take down little ole me. I'm honored." He gave a mock bow. "Too bad you're too big a pussy to try and take me out yourself," he taunted.

Satan took the barb and snarled. "I'd love nothing more than to take your head and mount it on my wall, but there are rules, boy."

Creed laughed, never taking his eyes off the threat in front of him. "Rules always matter to you. Not!"

Between one breath and the next the horde of demons disappeared.

"You are right. I am the ruler of all the Underworld. I can make the rules. Who says I can't decide who lives and dies?"

Satan stood, all sign of negligent pasha gone. "You want to fight me?" He tossed his head back and laughed.

"I will do you one better. I'll offer my life for theirs. Allow them to go back to their realm unharmed, and you can have me."

Before he could say a word, a small figure entered from the side. Her ghostly figure reminded him of Kyrene, only he saw goodness in her, where there was none in the other demon.

"Nay, I will not allow this."

Satan narrowed his eyes. "You have no say."

She smiled. "You will allow all of them to go, and I will," she swallowed before continuing. "I will give you two more years, Father. Two years and then I will be gone. You have that time to find my mom."

"Who are you?" Creed moved toward the newcomer, then froze as she held her hand up.

"I am Live, your Halfling, Kyrene's Halfling as well. You will do as I have bartered and go with your Chosen." A shudder wracked her small frame.

"I agree to your proposition."

"No," Creed roared, his eyes begged for her to not agree, knowing it was too late. Where was his own mother? She could save them all without this tiny scrap of a being offering up her existence to Satan.

"Why, Live?" He felt as if a thousand chains held him in place.

Live walked up to him, not an ounce of fear showed on her face. "My name is Live because nobody thought I would survive. I remember my mother's words to me." She leaned up on her toes. "You shouldn't be alive. Since you live that is your name demon. Then she tossed me into a pit, and left me. When Kyrene found me, I was a few days old. She made sure I had the things I needed to survive. I am Live, nothing else matters. Now, let them go, or the deal is off the table."

"Be gone, Creed, and know if I find you back here, you will be mine." Satan waved his hand, already dismissing them.

Live's clear blue eyes flashed triumph as she smiled at him. "Goodbye, Creed. Be well for both of us."

"I'll get you free, Live. I'll find your mother and make it so." It was a vow he would keep.

The dark look Satan sent his way would have wilted a lesser man. Creed raised his middle finger, backing toward Raina and the others. He felt her reaching out to him during his battles, but didn't want her to feel the pain he'd been in through their bond. A bright light burst into the dark chamber, scattering the carcasses of the dead.

"You dare try to harm my child, Lucifer?" Creed's mother floated above the ground, her form almost too bright to look at.

The sound of shattering stone had Creed's head whipping toward the throne, only to stare at the remains of what used to be part of Satan's solid black chair. The arms had been turned to dust from where his father had squeezed too tightly.

His mother's wings spread out, creating a barrier between them and Satan. "Live, come here, child."

Satan raised a black claw, his power raising the temperature. "She has made a bargain with me, and we have agreed."

"Since there is no contract signed, no blood has been spilled or given to seal the deal, she is still free. Come here, Live."

The command was followed by his mother's will being forced out, and Live was moved by an unseen hand. "You knew if you harmed my Creed, I would have the ability to do unto you, what you've done to him. You've harmed him by killing his sibling. Now, I will take him and his sibling out of here without recourse. Good day, Lucy."

Black smoke boiled from all around the dais where Satan lounged, but he didn't say a word. Creed saw the hatred burn in his black eyes, then he sat back with a heavy sigh. "This is not over, my dear."

"Of course it isn't. Good and evil will always battle, but the good will always prevail. However, you mess with my son again, and I'll bring down a contingent of angels, the likes of which you won't survive, and my son will sit on that throne. Remember that the next time you get a hair up your...you know what."

She raised her golden wings and then they were no longer in Hell, but back in the Fey world, with Live at their sides. The female had long silver blonde hair that reached her ass, with silver eyes. She was hauntingly beautiful.

"Mother, what the Hell were you thinking showing up there? He could have trapped you there?" Creed pulled his mother into his arms, careful not to hug her too tightly.

"My sweet child, always worried about hurting me," she whispered, patting his back.

He lifted her off the ground. "You are much frailer than he and I, of course I worry."

Looking over his shoulder she winked, then sent him flying through the air, her wings carrying them. "I am no delicate freaking flower, Creed."

Raina was pretty sure she was going to hyperventilate, or pass out. Probably both as she watched mother and son fly off. She'd endured the trauma of seeing the man, or demon, or whatever you wanted to call Creed be beaten so severely she was sure he'd be killed, only to watch him come out the victor time and time again. And if that wasn't enough, his bastard of a father upped the stakes and was ready to consume his soul in order to set them free, and Creed was going to do it, the sacrificial asshat. Goddess, she loved the man.

"It's amazing, isn't it," Live whispered.

She jerked at the husky words spoken next to her. Looking up, she was startled at the beauty that was Creed's half-sister. No way could she call her a Halfling. Kyrene must've had some good qualities to her since she did raise the younger woman, demon, or whatever Live was. As she continued to stare at the odd silver eyes, she realized she hadn't answered. "Yes, it is. I mean, a freaking angel in real life."

Live nodded. "Creed is half angel you know."

A blush stole up her neck, heating her face. She'd done all kinds of dirty things with an angel. Holy shit, was that even a legal thing to do?

"You're thinking naughty things aren't you? Don't deny it. I've seen more than my fair share to know when someone is or isn't."

"I'm going to Hell." She covered her face with both hands.

"Nah, not for that," Live said deadpan.

"Excuse me, but can someone explain why I have an angel and a demon flying around my forest? Wait a minute. Did that really just come out of my mouth? Oh God, I think I have a fever. Someone get a thermometer." Jenna glanced around at the group of people. "Now, I know everyone, but the angel, and the angel/mix. So, who are you?" She pointed her finger at Live.

Live blinked at Jenna. "Who's the sprite?"

Jenna put her hands on her hips. "Did she call me a sprite? Someone get my ladle. Nessie will show her who's a sprite."

Silver eyes flashed to red. "I don't like killing, but you sic your Nessie on me, and I'll do it."

A flick of her fingers, and Jenna held a kitchen utensil in her hand that had a strange looking end. "This is Nessie, child."

"You plan to attack me with a...what the fuck is that anyhow?" Live's eyes returned to the odd silver.

Jenna sniffed. "Have you never heard of the Loch Ness Monster?"

Raina put her hand up. "Live is Creed's half-sister, and has lived her life in Hell. I'm pretty sure they have many monsters there, but the Loch Ness isn't one of them."

Eyes as wide as saucers, Jenna tossed her ladle aside, then wrapped her arms around Live. "Oh, you poor sweet child. Come, let Mama Jenna make you something to eat and get you settled. You must be tired after your journey."

Live looked over her shoulder, shock and a little fear showed in her eyes.

"Jenna, we need to talk." Her brother Damien moved in front of them.

"I know, but not today. I have things to figure out. Many issues to settle." The ground beneath their feet rolled, sending Damien and Lucas sprawling backward. "You two need to go back to Earth, along with you, young Kellen. Your mate has been screaming in my head for days. Do you know it's All Hallows Eve, and the Iron Wolves are hosting a party? Do you know that Bodhi has gone missing and your sister is bent on chasing him down, whether he wants her to or not?"

Kellen growled, the sound sending a shiver up Raina's spine. "Send me home, Jennaveve."

"Since you asked so nicely, Kellen. Give Laikyn a kiss for me." Jenna snapped her fingers, and then Kellen was gone.

She turned to Live. "Stay here, Livey."

"I am not an animal to be told what to do." Live's eyes flashed red.

Jenna stood on her toes. "Don't make me angry, little girl."

She turned, giving Live her back. Raina prepared to defend the Fey, but Live was as stunned as she.

Damien and Lucas lumbered to their feet. Their fangs showing in clear anger. "Give me time. I am not asking, I'm telling. If you don't you will lose me." Instead of going up on her toes like she'd done to the others, her brother Lucas lifted their Hearts Love, then turned around.

Raina wanted to give the trio a bit of privacy while her body ached for Creed.

Creed and his mother landed between Live and Raina, his wounds completely healed.

"Hello, Raina. My son has told me all about you."

Feeling a whole lot out of place, Raina wasn't sure if she should curtsy, or not. Instead she nodded. "Um, it's very nice to meet you, Creed's mother."

"You are probably wondering many things, and for that I wish I had more time to explain. For now, how about I tell you that I love my son very much, and you may call me Lillianna. I must go, but Creed knows he can call on me. It may take me a bit to get to him, but I will come."

Lillianna gave her a kiss, and then she was gone.

"Holy shit, I just met an angel. Your mother is an angel." Raina held her hand over the spot where she'd been kissed.

Creed moved in front of her. "Hey, why don't you get that awed when I kiss you?"

She blinked up at him. "Your mother is a freaking angel."

He nodded. "You said that already."

"I hate to break this up, but you two need to go. Live is going to stay with me while she gets acclimated." Jenna walked over to them.

Raina looked over to where her brothers had been, but didn't see any sign of them. "Where are Damien and Lucas?"

Sadness welled in Jenna's eyes. "They are at your parent's home. Now, I just need to send you two back, and I will be able to rest. Live will be able to contact you and vice versa, but traveling back and forth will need to be arranged."

"Are you okay with those arrangements?" He asked Live.

Live nodded. "Your mother thinks it's a good idea for now."

Raina was going to ask when she'd spoken to Lillianna, but figured the angel had her ways. "Thank you, Jenna, for your hospitality. Don't keep my brothers waiting too long."

Jenna inclined her head. "See you soon, Raina."

Live looked at Creed, then at the grass beneath their feet.

"Give me a moment with my sisterkin." He placed a kiss where his mother had on Raina's cheek, the warmth spread to her heart.

Chapter Eight

Creed eliminated the space between him and Live, still unable to believe this being was willing to give up her life, or at least two years, which would have felt like an eternity, for him. He knew why Satan wanted his life. To consume even the small amount of light within him, Satan would have access to Earth, and possibly other realms in his own form. He'd clearly taken Raina knowing she was his Chosen, knowing Creed would sell his immortal soul to the Devil himself to save her.

Stopping in front of Live, he took a deep breath. "Thank you for what you were willing to do for me. Had I known about you, I'd have ensured your safety the same as Kyrene. I'm sorry I didn't do better for you."

His hands itched to hold her. Kyrene never allowed him to do such, the demon was more Hate Demon, but she'd allowed him to provide the comforts he could, and wanted to learn how to defend herself.

"Kyrene said you wouldn't want another dependent. She said I was her burden to raise, and I had to hide whenever you came near." Her liquid silver eyes lifted to meet his, hurt radiated up at him.

He shook his head. "She lied. I'd have taken care of you. I'd have offered you everything I could." He had to swallow. "You have a goodness in you she never had. I don't understand how she hid that from me."

Live gave a mirthless laugh. "She was very good at lying. Not to mention you were easy to hear when you were near. She would summon me and send me to the deepest pits of Hell, and cover me with things best left unmentioned." A shudder wracked her frail frame.

Unable to stop himself, he lifted one hand and cradled her cheek in his palm. "I am sorry."

A lone tear leaked from the corner of her eye. When she didn't pull away from his touch, he decided to say fuck the past and Kyrene's aversion to his affection. "Can I hug you? A brotherly hug?"

"I've never had a hug." Live lifted her head from his hand.

He made sure he didn't crush her bones as he wrapped both arms around her, again shocked at the fact he had a sisterkin who wasn't filled with darkness. "I will make sure this is the first of many, sister."

"I think I like that better than Halfling," she whispered shyly.

Sitting her back on her feet, he used his thumbs to wipe away the moisture from beneath her eyes. "Me too, Livey."

Her eyes squinted. "You are the second to call me that. First that Jenna person, now you. What is that?"

"That is a nickname. And, it suits you better than just Live. Although Live shows you are worthy of the name, because it takes a strong soul to survive where we were born and brought up. You are beautiful inside and out. Livey, is what I will call you, if that is okay?" He wasn't sure what he'd do if she said no.

A nod was his answer. "I think I like that. I will still call you Creed. It means faith. You were the one thing I believed was good even though Kyrene tried to tell me otherwise. I knew if you did all you did for her, you couldn't truly be that bad. I had complete faith you would save me too."

If he could, he'd go back and...no, he still would take care of Kyrene, she was his Halfling. He couldn't, wouldn't be able to look at her as he did Livey, but she was still his blood. "I will be back, and you can contact me through Jenna. Try not to...well, try to get along with the Fey, she's different, but good."

Livey's eyes went to where Jenna and Raina stood staring out toward the purple and pink sky. "I think we'll get along just fine. The ladle named Nessie? She tilted her head in question. "We shall see. I have seen many monsters, that one doesn't scare me at all."

He gave her another hug, kissing the top of her head. "If I could erase it all I would."

"What doesn't kill you makes you stronger." Livey stepped away, holding her head high.

They both began walking back to the other two women. "Then we are both made of the strongest stuff then," Creed agreed.

"Hey you two. We were just thinking we should cop a squat out here and count the cows jumping over the moon," Jenna pointed at the sky.

Sure enough, Creed watched as a couple cows appeared to jump over a moon. Livey gasped as Raina clapped her hand over her mouth.

"Alright you crazy Fey, send us home." Creed wrapped his arm around Raina, needing to feel her wrapped around him.

"See how you are? Fine, be gone with your bad self." Jenna flicked her hand.

Creed held Raina as the world spun, and then he found himself back at his home.

"Wow, she is a little crazy, but I love her," Raina joked.

"I love you more." He bent and kissed her upturned face.

"I'm more of a show, than tell kind of girl." She rubbed against him.

He didn't need her to tell him twice, his body aching for hers worse than any wound he'd ever suffered. A cough had him taking a deep breath before he did something he'd regret, knowing his staff would have known the minute they'd returned.

"Holly, could you let everyone know my Chosen and I will be busy for the next long while. I will summon you when we need something. Until then, enjoy some time off." He opened his eyes and met the amused stare of his housekeeper.

"Yes, Sire. If you should need anything, let us know." Holly and her mate turned away, efficient as ever.

With a nod, he flashed them to his bedroom. Rude? Maybe...but it had been too long since he'd made love to Raina. Too long since he'd felt her flesh under his. Too long, and he needed, wanted to rectify that error sooner, rather than later.

"I'd say that wasn't the politest thing, but we'll make it up to them later. Much, later." Raina gasped, her eyes going down to their nakedness. "Now, this I could totally get used to."

"Your wish is my command." Her fingers brushed down the front of his chest and he had to suppress a shudder.

Her hand gripped his cock, no shy virgin, the little minx moved her palm up and down, rubbing her thumb over the tip. Pre-come leaking out, she smoothed it over the head, then glanced up at him. "I love the way you taste."

Eyes cloudy with lust, Raina almost unmanned him as she licked her lips, making his breaths come out in pants like an untried youth. Something he couldn't remember ever being. "Sweetheart, if I let you wrap those lips around me, I'll come in two seconds flat."

Moving her hand up and down in a faster, jerkier motion, she panted. "And that is a bad thing, how?"

He put his hand over hers, stopping the motion of her fingers. "The next time I come, it will be inside my Chosen. I'm going to claim you tonight. Fully." He let her see his intent.

The scent of her arousal spiked the air. His hips pumped against her hand involuntarily, but he didn't want her to jack him off, although it felt amazing.

The large bed in the middle of the room had beautiful views out the floor to ceiling windows at night, but on this evening, he didn't think anything would be lovelier than Raina.

"Tonight, I make you mine," he said, his voice deep with a need he couldn't mask.

She shook her head. "I've been yours since the first time."

He lifted her, placing her in the middle of the bed, settling between her thighs. Eyes locked, breaths hitched, he took her lips in a kiss he swore took his soul. His cock slid against her center, but he held back, paying reverence to her mouth. Raina moaned into his mouth, her tongue worked in and out of his like he wanted to do with his cock.

Breaking away from her, he rose onto his knees. He brushed his knuckles down the center of her chest, feeling her heart race beneath them. "Are you nervous?"

"I want to bond with you completely, but what about the consequences?" she asked.

"My mother has assured me we are compatible in every way. My blood will not hurt you or vice versa." He smiled. "Not that I ever feared yours would harm me."

His hand slipped further down, tracing the indent of her belly button. "I have fantasized about what it would be like to take you completely. If you want to wait, I will." It would kill him, but he would for her.

Raina shook her head, her hand grabbing his and pressing it against her mound. "Goddess, no. Claim me in every way, and I will you. I already have in my heart."

His other hand cupped her breast and tweaked a nipple. "No going back, Mon Eros."

"Please...I need you..." Raina moaned as he slipped a finger through her wet lips, plunging a thick digit into her, making her cry out.

"Fuck, you are wet." He pumped another finger inside her.

Raina clutched at his wrist, her head tossed back and forth.

"I'm going to make you come with my fingers, then I'm going to fill you with my cock, and my fangs as I claim you as my Chosen."

"Yes, Creed. I need you so much," she cried.

He flicked his thumb over her clit while pumping his fingers in and out, adding a third digit, watching her face as he took her up hard and fast. The feel of her pussy clamping down along with the rosy hue to her skin signaled her impending release. His head bent, sucking a hardened nipple into his mouth, sending her that final bit over the edge.

Raina's back arched, violent spasms shook her so hard she nearly dislodged him from between her legs. He continued to pump in and out of her, prolonging her climax, then without pausing, he withdrew his fingers, making her whimper in protest.

"Love you to the ends of all the realms and back, Raina," he whispered lining his cock up to her entrance. The spike of her unique arousal filled him with pride as he slowly entered her until he was seated to the hilt inside his Chosen. His mind searched for hers, needing that connection.

The sweetness that was Raina opened for him. The overwhelming feel of being stretched to the limit, almost bordering on pain had him holding completely still. "Are you okay?" he asked.

"Absolutely. Don't move just yet. I love the feel of having all of you in me." She squeezed her inner walls.

"Ah fuck...don't do that...damn it. Too fucking good." He groaned.

She laughed, the sound like silver bells. "What's wrong?"

He pulled out and plunged back in, one hand holding her hip in place while he lifted her leg over his other, opening her up more fully. "If you don't stop doing that, I'll be forced to exert my authority over you and do something. I don't know what, cause you've short-circuited my brain cells."

His breath heaved out of his lungs as he slid in and out faster than he wanted.

"I'm sorry. I'll behave," she gasped.

Creed swiveled his hips, brushing against her clit on each downward thrust. When talking became impossible for each of them, he knew he was doing something right. Her body began to quiver beneath him, tightening around his cock. He began pounding into her harder, making sure he hit all her pleasure points. Needing to kiss her, sealing their entire beings together, he took her lips in a forceful kiss, demanding everything from her, desperation riding him.

When he felt his orgasm racing toward him, he broke away from her mouth. "Raina Cordell, I am not good enough for you, but I will do everything in my power to be. From the first time I saw you, I knew you were mine. I claim you as my Chosen, my heart, my soul belongs to you." His fangs lengthened, waiting for her assent.

Piercing blue eyes locked with his. "Do it, Creed, my Hearts Love. For I claim you for my very own as well." She turned her head, and guided his head to her throat.

Just as his orgasm slammed into him, he sank his fangs into her throat. The small exchange of her lifesblood filled him, her light lifting him higher, making him feel whole for the first time in thousands of years. He sealed the small punctures.

Hips still thrusting, ecstasy still rolling through him, he rolled to his back and presented his neck. Raina wasted no time, her eyes gone red. When her fangs sank into him, his cock jerked, and he swore more come spilled as his eyes rolled to the back of his head. He shouted her name until she went limp on top of him, both overcome with pleasure.

"Raina," he said holding her tightly.

Her heart beat the same rhythm as his, just as it should for all eternity. He pressed his lips to her temple.

"I can't wait to tell my parents."

His body froze. "I've never met a female of worth's parents before." He wasn't sure what they'd think of him. Maybe since he'd saved his Chosen's mother, therein giving them all the chance at a happy life he'd be a shoe in.

She patted his chest. "They'll love you just like I do."

That was to be seen, but as long as he had her, he'd deal with whatever was thrown at them.

Raina closed her eyes on a sigh. She could hear the wheels spinning in her dark lover's mind. Creed was always expecting others to hurt or reject him. Well, she would make sure he knew she would never do that, and would make damn sure nobody ever would, or face her wrath if they ever did.

"We'll go see my family tomorrow. Best to rip the band-aid off quickly, than to do it in slow increments." She kissed his smooth pec, amazed he showed no scars from his battles.

"My mother healed me while we flew together. She is amazing."

Lifting her head she blinked up at him. "You reading my mind?"

He winked. "We are linked now. You'll have to build some walls if you want to block me."

She shook her head. "I have no secrets."

Two days, and many orgasms later...

"Maybe you should have come alone," Creed muttered.

Raina laughed, charmed her mate was nervous to meet her mom and dad. "They are going to love you, I promise." He'd explained his past with her parents after they'd bonded the first time, and although she'd had a moment of unease that he'd thought her mother was his Chosen, it was quickly dispelled as she'd looked into his mind. There was no denying the fact he hadn't truly loved her mother. Nor that his love for her was all encompassing, and she returned it tenfold.

"I wouldn't bet on that," growled Damikan.

"Daddy," Raina squealed and launched herself into the waiting arms of her father.

"How is my baby girl?" The Vampire King held Raina for a moment, his eyes soft until they landed on Creed.

She sighed. "Wonderful. I know you felt it when we bonded, but I want you to formally meet my mate Creed."

Creed bowed at them both. "It's good to see you again, Damikan, and you are looking as gorgeous as always, Luna."

Her father looked stunned for a moment, then he smiled. "You have more light in you than the last time I saw you."

Luna slapped his shoulder, then walked past her mate. "Welcome to the family, Creed." She kissed Creed on both cheeks, making her own mate growl.

Raina giggled. "Dad, you really need to learn to stop doing that. You are sounding more wolfish every day."

Her father gave a playful bite, then he too moved forward to shake Creed's hand.

"Well, since it is All Hallows Eve, I guess anything is possible, even me turning into a wolf on the full moon." He winked at his mate, then pulled her away from Creed, and to his side.

Nobody could deny the possessive way each man held their mates, nor the fact each one could be considered dark in their own way. Raina smiled up at Creed, letting him see and feel her love. Her heart melted as he embraced her and his lips kissed her temple in front of her parents. He had the power to crush her with not only his body, but his mind and heart. However, she knew that he'd give his life to keep her safe. A small tear escaped as she realized she had exactly what she'd always craved. A dark lover worthy of every girl's dreams.

The End

Bodhi's Synful Mate

Iron Wolves Book 6
Blurb

KARSYN STYLES... aka Syn is tired of waiting on the man she knows is her mate to claim her. She's going to take matters into her own hands, even if that means teaching the stubborn wolf she's more than just the alpha's baby sister.

BODHI... has fought the feelings he has for the little wolf who's supposed to be like a sister to him. Only the feelings she's stirred in his body and heart are far from brotherly. He's done everything in his power to keep her at a distance, even going against everything he and his wolf want, but nothing can tame either man or beast except the one female meant to be theirs.

Just when he is ready to claim his mate, Bodhi's world is rocked as his past comes back with a vengeance. He wasn't born a wolf, but turned when his family was slaughtered. He'd thought he was all alone in the human world, grateful for his wolven family, until one fateful encounter.

Syn sees the man she loves pulling away. Her heart can't take another rejection, or seeing him turn to another female for the comfort only she should be giving him. She'll do anything to show him they're meant to be together.

Neither realize the danger lurking in the shadows as Bodhi's past is more sinister than either realize. Can the Iron Wolves survive what's coming next, or will what destroyed Bodhi's past come back to do the same to their future?

Bodhi's Synful Mate
Adult Excerpt

Bodhi controlled the urge to lift up and power into her. He needed to make her come before he shoved his cock into the tightest, sweetest pussy on earth and beyond. When he'd said she smelled like sin and spice, he meant it. She tasted like the sweetest cinnamon and sugar mixture he'd ever had. He wanted to gorge himself on her flavor. Taking his time, he held her down while she bucked against him, her cries were like music to his ears, a thunderous roar like a heavy metal band drumming in his head. His cock had been hard since he'd walked in her door. No, it had been hard for years, but now it throbbed like the primal beast he was.

He took his time, worshipping every inch of her, telling her how perfect she was without words, letting her feel how much she meant to him, only her for the rest of their lives. If he could, he'd stay right where he was, but his dick ached, demanding release. She was close to coming, and he wanted to feel that, needed to make her shatter. He wanted to watch her come apart for him. He hadn't lied when he'd told her he wanted to memorize the exact moment for all eternity. Watching her dazed and sated face ranked right up there with the best of the best for him.

Her hands went to his hair, pulling, telling him without words what she needed. Bodhi licked faster, worked his fingers inside her faster, drawing more of her flavor into himself. "That's it. Trust me. Give it to me. Come, now." He lashed at her clit, suckled it and then drew it into his mouth. When her inner muscles began to squeeze his fingers, he looked up and watched her come apart, felt the ripples and couldn't wait to feel them working his cock. Fuck, she was beautiful when she came.

He rose above her, and her eyes were slumberous, but still needy.

His cock was hard, and thick, pulsing precome. He ran a hand up and down it, then settled between her spread thighs. "You ready, chérie?"

Tight. So damn tight and hot. He positioned the head of his dick at the entrance to heaven and waited.

"Yes, make me yours."

"You've always been mine," he growled. The broad head slid into her silken depths, her heat licked him.

"Mine," her whispered words made him smile.

His breath left him on a hiss. "Fuck yes, yours." Somehow his lungs remembered to work, and although he wanted, needed to plunge into her silken depths, he took it slow, driving in an inch at a time. Every slow measured thrust he could feel the ache in his balls to come boiling up. Shit, at this rate he'd come as soon as he was buried into the hilt.

With his eyes locked on her blue ones, he kept focused on her for any sign of pain. The walls of her pussy still contracted from her orgasm, rippling along his shaft, and every inch he gained felt like a tight fist squeezing him. As he finally pushed all the way in, he settled over her, his gaze clinging to hers. He loved the way she met him eye-to-eye. The way she looked at him as if he hung the moon. Goddess, he prayed he never fucked up.

"Damn, I swear, you are the sweetest thing I've ever seen in all my life. How did I get so lucky," he breathed out reverently. Truth rang out. His fingers flexed on her hips from where he held her still for his deep penetration, not wanting her to move just yet out of fear he'd come before he was ready. "You're so tight. Your body was made for me, and I for you. Do you feel that?" He pulled out and pressed back in. "One day, we will create children when you're ready. Our loving will make a part of you and me."

She cried out and thrashed beneath him, trying to get him to move. "You can't say shit like that and not move. Need to come."

Bending, he took her mouth in a demanding kiss, then moved to her shoulder, knowing he was going to claim her in the way of their wolves as well. The mating mark would be visible for all their kind to see, and he couldn't wait. At the moment of her climax, he planned to claim her there. He licked the spot, bit down, but not hard enough to break the skin then eased back. Her blues eyes lit up.

His cock was buried deep, ready to explode. "Are you okay?" He'd seen the flash of pain in her face as he'd entered her.

The beautiful flush that covered her skin enchanted him. Hell, Bodhi couldn't believe he was thinking such things, yet with his mate beneath him, the flowery words were perfect for how he was feeling. When she didn't answer, he lifted his hands and grabbed both of hers, pulling them next her head. "I asked you a question." Steel entered his voice.

Syn swallowed. "It only hurt a few seconds."

He opened his mind and entered only the front of hers to gauge her words. Seeing the honesty there, he nodded. In the position they were now in, he was in complete control, and he loved it. He gave her a grin. At a glance down, her hair had spilled across the silver sheets, its dark mass a stark contrasts of silk on silk. He fucking loved her. Not like a brother, or a pack member. A mate's love.

"I truly am okay, Bo. Please move." Her words were accompanied by her squeezing the inner muscles of her pussy.

The delicious sensations had him pulling back and moving forward, the action nearly strangling his cock, building him up to the best orgasm of his life. He slammed deeper, harder than he'd planned, but she met him stroke for stroke. Their shifter strength allowed them to take each other harder, faster, and he pounded into her like he'd never allowed himself to do with another. Every stroke jolted the bed, made her breast bounce, and he held her hands next to her head, his body in complete control of hers. She was completely held down by him. All his.

Completely lost to making love to his mate, he didn't realize how close she was to shattering until her body clamped down on him, and then he had to exert his iron control to keep from following her. He didn't want to come just yet. The need to push her over the precipice and watch her come apart rode him. "Come for me again," he ordered. Two more times he instructed her, holding her down, commanding her to come, before he allowed himself the pleasure of coming. When he did, his wolf came to the surface, and his canines lengthened. The area he'd chosen beckoned. Streaks of fire raced from his spine to his balls, and as he allowed himself to come, the arcs of pleasure raced through his system, he struck.

Syn's eyes widened, her pleas grew louder and her breath hitched as he claimed her. Another orgasm rolled over her. The spasming of her pussy forced another from him, making his head light, his abs quiver, and if he'd been standing he was sure his legs would've gone out. Giving his life new meaning. Giving him new life. He and Syn became one. He released her neck with a gentle lick, and turned his throat, giving her access, and jerked as she bit down on him in a much daintier bite, yet every bit as possessive, claiming.

Bodhi's Synful Mate
Story Excerpt

The constant need to be filled by Bodhi seemed to have eased after their last violent lovemaking session against the wall. Staring at herself in the mirror of her bathroom, Syn touched one of the marks on her hips, shivering at the remembered feel of his possession. Holy fucking shit, Lyric didn't mention it would be so intense when she mated. The thought of her best friend had her looking for her cell. She glanced at the clock, and quickly walked back into her recently re-made bed. Each step was a reminder of Bodhi's possession as she felt a slight twinge between her thighs. With her shifter abilities, if she was to shift to her wolf, and then back to human, all her injuries would be healed, but she was loathe to do so. Gah, she was so screwed.

She swiped across the screen and hit the button for Lyric. The ringtone her friend chose for herself, had her smiling as she waited.

"Hello, beotch. How's the mating going?" Lyric asked.

Syn shook her head. "Oh, we've been fucking like bunnies, and then we fucked some more. Would you like all the down and dirty details?"

The sound of Lyric groaning, and Rowan yelling at her to take the phone off of speaker made Syn blush and look around for Bodhi. "Dang it you hussy, why didn't you tell me you weren't alone?"

Lyric's laughing voice almost had Syn jumping into her truck, and racing over there to knock her best friend in the head.

"Oh Goddess, you should have seen Rowan's face. Now that, is what we call free entertainment." Lyric laughed some more, then stopped as she must've realized Syn wasn't laughing with her. "Oh, hun, I'm sorry. You know I didn't mean to upset you. Hell, I tell you everything, even when Rowan's right in the room.

He sort of knows everything anyways. He's like Super-SEAL, or would that be WolfieSEAL? Shit, what is he anyway now?"

"Lyric, shut up. You're gonna give me a headache. Rowan is...Rowan. Who happens to be your mate. He's an ex-SEAL but he's also a shifter, so I guess he's all that and a bag of chips. But, that doesn't mean I want him privy to my sex life."

Lyric sniffed, and Syn had the impression her best friend was actually wiping away real tears. "Are you crying? You can't cry. You're the one who fucked up." Syn gentled her voice. Lyric never cried. "Do I need to come over there? Did Super-Wolfeal do something?"

"Wolfeal?" Lyric giggled.

"Yeah, I sort of came up with that. You know how Jenna and Kellen call the Cordell twins Wolpires, well Wolfeals. What do you think?"

"I'm totally gonna tell him his new nickname. Now, stop evading me, and spill. What did you and Bodhi talk about? I don't need the dirty dirty, since I'm a happily mated female, I kinda know what you do. Stick part A into slot A, B, or C."

Syn pulled the phone away from her ear. "So you're saying you allow Rowan to stick his dick into your vajayjay, your mouth and your..." she was cut off as Lyric screeched.

"Alright, that's enough girl talk while I'm in residence, damn wolf hearing," Rowan growled into the phone.

"Give me the phone back you big bully."

"I'll talk to you later, Lyric. Don't let the big bad Wolfeal get the better of you. Offer up part C," Syn said then hung up as Lyric squealed louder.

"You, Karsyn Styles, are a bad girl." Bodhi leaned against the doorjamb.

He looked too damn good for her peace of mind, but she kept that to herself. Although the smirk on his face let her know he'd read her mind. His eyes, those green emerald fire ones, looked at her with such tenderness, making her sigh. "Well, you bring out the bad in me."

Straightening, he strolled into the room. "I hate to leave you so soon, but I need to go talk with my sister, and Kellen. There's a lot of unfinished business with her...husband, and his family. We know Rodriguez wasn't in residence, which means he's still a threat."

Fear skittered through her. "He knows where we're located."

"Let him come here," he growled, then paced away from her to stare out the window. "I saw some of the things he did to her."

She didn't need to ask who *the her* was. When they'd connected, and their mate link clicked into place, she'd seen his memories that he hadn't blocked. She couldn't imagine the hell Layla had endured, only hoped that Jenna could help ease some of it. "What're you going to do?"

Bodhi sighed. "I'm going to hunt his ass down, and kill him. His entire family will die, if not by my hands, then by our pack. Kellen has given me his blessing as well as his assurance he wants to dismember them all slowly. He said Jenna was too lenient when she collapsed the home with the fuckers inside. I tend to agree with him." He smiled grimly.

Syn remained silent. The need for vengeance was one she understood, but her gut told her it wasn't going to be quite the easy task her mate thought. No, she didn't doubt for a minute her mate was a badass, however, the man they were facing wasn't an honorable man. She'd seen inside Layla's memories, things she wondered if Bodhi had truly paid attention to, or if he'd been too disturbed to notice the little things.

"Go ahead, say what's on your mind. I can see you have an opinion, and while I may not agree, I do value your wisdom."

"It's not my past to tell, but I suggest when you speak to your sister, you listen, and try not to freak the fuck out. She's suffered enough without her brother going apeshit on her. Not that I think you'll hurt her, but Layla is going to need you to stay calm while she tells you her tale." Syn held up a finger. "If she opens up enough to tell you that is. If not, then when you look into her mind, really look."

"What aren't you telling me? What did you see that I missed?" Bodhi came to stand in front of her, his hands holding her by the shoulders.

"I'm telling you to keep your shit cool, and don't be an ass." If it was possible, he seemed to grow without shifting. Hell, his entire body appeared to vibrate.

"I hate fucking riddles, and I most certainly don't like it when my mate won't just give me the deets I need, so I'm not walking into a minefield." Blunt, that was what Bodhi was.

Syn shook her head. "As your mate, and Layla's sister-in-law to be, I'm giving you both my respect. What I saw through your mind, wasn't a true vision of mine. It could be a distorted version, so back the fuck up off me." Mate or not, her wolf came to the surface, ready to protect them.

"The Dominguez family are, and were, vicious from what I saw. Hell, I was too young to really know anything, other than my friend Rod wasn't able to play on certain days because he was in trouble. What did I miss?" He closed his eyes for a couple minutes, then they opened wide. "From what I saw through my sister's mind, they not only killed, but they enjoyed it. The killing and torturing. Her husband made her watch. He got off on it. Shit, that's what you were trying to tell me. I missed it when I connected with Layla." He stared down at her, his heartbeat throbbed visibly though the vein in his neck.

"Yeah, I'm sure there's more." She licked her lips.

Mystic Wolves Book 1

Accidentally Wolf

"It's okay, little guy," Cora soothed, shoving down her fear for the little wolf caught in the illegal trap. The device had been hidden in a shallow crevice within a couple miles of her veterinary clinic. The way his wound was bleeding she knew, if she didn't get him free, he'd likely die. Inching closer to him, Cora watched for signs of aggression. "I'm going to get you out of there, but you have to promise not to bite me, okay?"

She squatted down until her face was almost level with his. "I'll try not to hurt you."

Cora swore it looked like the little guy nodded. At least Cora hoped that was a nod of agreement. His tiny body shook and shuddered. She prayed she wasn't mistaken.

After carefully looking over the contraption, she realized the jaws were meant for a much larger animal. Luckily for this wolf, his leg wasn't clamped between the steel jaws, only grazed. He was still stuck with his larger paw locked on the inside of the obviously modified bear trap and had a nasty gash that needed tending, sooner rather than later.

What seemed liked hours later, Cora finally got the device forced opened. Sweat trickling down her temples stung her eyes. The wolf lay panting like he'd just ran for miles. His gaze seemed to convey that he trusted her. Although it looked as though the trap only grazed his leg, she still checked to make sure it wasn't broken.

With a glance up at the darkening sky, Cora shrugged out of her jacket, leaving herself in only the yoga leggings and tank top she wore for her daily jog. South Dakota, during the day, could be warm, but as soon as the sun goes down, the temperatures drop dramatically. "Okay, little guy. I'm going to wrap you in my coat, and then I'm going to take you home with me."

Matching actions to words, she gently lifted his body. As she went to place his front right paw inside the jacket, the wolf howled the most pitiful whine, breaking her heart.

"I know it hurts, but I..." Cora jerked back in shock when the wounded animal bit down on her arm.

Once the wolf wriggled out of her coat, Cora watched in amazement as he licked her wound. If she didn't know any better, she'd swear he was apologizing, but thought that would be crazy. She gaped at him and scooted back a step or two, or three, until she stopped herself.

He whined again before trying to stand on his own, falling down when his front leg wouldn't hold him up.

Ignoring her own injury, she grabbed up her jacket and wrapped it around his body, being sure to pay close attention to his bleeding leg. "I know you're hurt, but try not to bite me again." She tried to sound stern when inside she was scared.

The walk back to her clinic took twice as long as normal since she didn't want to jar her patient any more than necessary. Every now and then his rough tongue would peek out and lick her arm. Although she was caught up on all her shots, she still worried about diseases from animals such as the wild wolf. At first glance she thought he was a baby wolf, now with him gathered in her arms and the couple of miles trek back to her home, she discovered he wasn't so young.

"Goodness, you must weigh close to seventy pounds, big guy."

Cora kept up a steady dialogue as she walked. When the clinic came into view, she nearly dropped to her knees in relief. Her arms shook under the stress of holding so much weight for such a long period of time. Normally, the hike would have taken her no time at all, but holding an injured animal that weighed almost as much as she did, the entire way was taxing, to say the least, not to mention the bite on her arm burned like fire.

She stopped outside the back door, adjusting her hold to punch in the code to unlock the back door, and, exhaling in relief, she murmured, "Thank you, technology." Cora's breathing was ragged by the time she made it inside.

Attached to the clinic was her small apartment, with a steel door separating the two spaces. Again, she punched in the code and then used her shoulder to enter the office area.

"Almost there, big guy. I'll have you fixed up in no time." Sweat poured down her chest, soaking her top. Cora ignored it all to focus on getting her patient fixed up. After she'd cleaned his wound, she found he had indeed broken his front leg, which was why he had probably bitten her when she moved him.

Thankful that her training kicked in to tend to the little wolf, when all she wanted to do was curl up in a ball and take a long nap, Cora placed the patched up wolf inside the padded kennel with a sense of relief. He whined when she attempted to lock the gate, his pain-filled gaze breaking her heart.

There were no other patients in the hospital area. She made the decision to leave the lock off, hoping she wasn't making a mistake and headed to take a bath.

Cora wiped her hand across the fogged mirror and stared at her own pain-filled gaze. "How can one little bitty bite hurt so damn much?" She looked at the freshly cleaned wound for what seemed like the thousandth time and stuck a thermometer in her mouth and waited for the beep, promising herself if her temperature was too high, she'd head into town.

Even after taking meds and a cool bath, nothing was bringing her temperature down. Looking at the triple digit reading on the tiny screen she cringed. There was nothing else she could do except head into town to urgent med. Cora really hated to go to the emergency room. She rolled her eyes and shook her head, stopping when the motion made her feel like she was on a tilt-a-whirl.

Wrapping a towel around herself, she decided to check on her patient one more time before she got dressed. The door between her home and the clinic was open, but the lights were out, sending a shiver of fear down her spine. Cora flipped the switch on the wall, illuminating the walkway. Her head felt heavy, the lights overly bright, making her stumble and lose her footing.

"Shit, damn." Rising to her feet, she reached her palm out to the wall to help steady herself and blinked a few times to bring things back into focus.

Standing in the middle of her clinic, with the injured wolf in his hands, was the most magnificent man she'd ever seen in her entire life. At over six foot tall, with short blonde hair and tattoos—lots of tattoos. The man exuded sex and menace. Yes, he definitely looked like he was angry. Even with her head feeling wonky, the sight of the unknown man made her body come alive. A whole different pulse began beating between her thighs, making Cora want to reach out and touch him, and not because she was in fear for her life.

"Who are you, and why do you have my wolf?" Cora was happy her voice didn't come out sounding as scared as she felt.

"Your wolf?"

The big man growled, the sound making her feel things she really shouldn't. Her nipples peaked at his deep rumble. Cora blamed the reaction on the fever.

"Listen, despite the fact you obviously broke into my clinic and I could press charges, I won't, but only if you put the animal down and leave the same way you came. You have less than five minutes, and then my offer is gone." Cora arched an eyebrow at him. "Do we have a deal?"

She waited for him to agree and put the sleeping wolf back down. Instead he quirked an eyebrow of his own, widened his stance, and sniffed the air.

In a move too fast for Cora to comprehend, the hunk standing a good ten feet away from her one moment, was all of a sudden crowding her space, sniffing her neck.

"Hey, have you heard of personal space?" When Cora attempted to push him back, her world spun.

Zayn Malik didn't know whether to laugh or growl at the human who tried to tell him what to do, all while she stood in nothing but a miniscule towel. Holding his nephew in wolf form, he opted for the latter. Every member of their pack knew the rules, and he couldn't imagine Nolan, even at the young age of seven, breaking them. He'd wait until whatever drugs the woman gave Nolan wore off, and his nephew could shift back to find out what happened.

The overwhelming scent of antiseptic clouded his senses, making it hard for him to discern the unusual smells assaulting him. When she raised her hand to push him back, he watched her eyes roll back in her head. Zayn shifted Nolan to one arm, being careful of his injured leg, and caught the woman in his other arm.

That was how his alpha found him, holding an injured cub in one arm and a naked female in the other. It wasn't his fault the towel was dislodged when he pulled her into his arm to stop her from face planting onto the ceramic tile floor.

"You want to tell me why you are holding my cub and an unconscious naked human, Zayn?"

The smile his brother suppressed didn't make Zayn happy. He wanted to toss the human to Niall. Only fear of hurting his nephew kept him from following through on the thought. "Fuck off, Niall," he grumbled.

"Give me Nolan. Do we know what happened to him?" Niall reached for his cub, carefully tucking him into his body.

As he handed Nolan over to Niall, Zayn watched his brother grimace at the bandage on his son's leg, then sniff at the offending thing like he wanted to rip it off. The joking man was gone, replaced by the concerned father. Niall stood at over six foot three with more red in his blonde hair, but with the same blue eyes Zayn had. When Niall spoke as alpha, everyone in the pack listened. Although they had pack mates who were bigger than Niall, none could take him in a fight in human or wolf form.

They'd come to the Mystic River Pack in South Dakota when Niall found his mate by chance during one of their annual bike rides to Sturgis. Within a few months they'd found themselves full-fledged members of the pack, and Niall had learned he was to become a father.

His brother's nose then turned to the woman Zayn cradled in his arms. Niall's face got too close for Zayn's peace of mind to a bandage wrapped around her thin arm, making his inner wolf rumble close to the surface.

"Do you smell that?" Niall sniffed again.

"What?" Zayn pulled the woman closer to his chest, using his large hand to cover as much of her bare ass from his brother as possible.

The right side of Niall's mouth quirked up for a moment before he turned serious. He bent to pick up the towel that had been dropped and draped it over the female.

"She's been bitten."

Narrowing his eyes, Zayn ran his gaze over the sleeping woman. "What did you say?"

The woman in his arms stirred, a feverish light in her eyes. That was when he noticed she was extremely hot to the touch. The smell of the clinic and the medicines had masked the unmistakable scent of the marking, which meant his sweet little nephew had bitten the good doctor when she had obviously tried to help him.

"You smell soooo delicious." Cora licked her lips.

"Um, what's your name, sweetheart?" Zayn tilted his head back from her questing lips and tongue. *Damn, her tongue is really long.*

"Mmm. You taste really good too." Another wet swipe from her tongue had him panting.

"Oh, goddess. Baby, you need to stop." Zayn needed to get the woman to stop licking him or he was going to throw her down on the table and fuck her.

How the hell did she go from being cradled in his arms, to wrapped around him with her legs locked around his hips, and her arms around his head? Zayn swallowed. Jesus, he was ready to come in his jeans with his brother and nephew not five feet away.

"That's enough, Cora." The low timber of Niall's voice reverberated around the room. A shiver went through the woman in his arms, and she swung her stare toward his brother.

Niall held an ID card with a picture of the woman in his arms. The name, Dr. Cora Welch, was at the top for Zayn to see. His brother grinned, his blue eyes dancing with mirth.

Cora's pussy contracted. Holy crap, the man was hot with a capital oh-my-lawd H, and she was humping him like a cat in heat, a naked cat in fricking heat.

She unlocked her ankles from the blonde Adonis's waist, hoping her legs would hold her up. They wobbled but didn't buckle—thankfully. "I'm so sorry...I don't know what came over me."

"I know what almost came all over me."

Sucking in a swift breath, Cora crossed one arm over her breasts and snatched the towel from the red haired man. Not that they hadn't seen everything there was to see, but she was in control of herself now.

"Smooth, Zayn, smooth. I apologize for my brother. He's not usually so crass, but we were worried when we couldn't find our little one here." He indicated the now alert wolf.

Eyes so blue peeked out between the big man's arms, accompanied by the whine she'd become accustomed to from the cub. She reached an unsteady hand toward his head to give a little scratch between his ears.

"Luckily for him, he's going to be okay. I found him stuck in a medieval looking animal trap made for a much larger animal. His little leg here," she indicated his cast, "barely missed being snapped in half by the steel jaws. I set the break and cleaned the wound. He should be right as rain in a few weeks."

Here she was buck-ass naked, carrying on a conversation with two men and a wolf. She was definitely sick. Cora raised her hand to feel her head. The short speech made her breathless, like she'd just run a marathon.

Behind her, she heard something growl. Turning to see the gorgeous man wearing a scowl, she took an involuntary step away. She looked around, fearing a wild animal had somehow gotten inside her office.

"Thank you, Cora Welch, for saving my cub. I owe you a life debt."

She swung her gaze back to the man holding the wolf. "Who are you? I've seen you in town, but I don't think we've met."

"I am Niall Malik. The man behind you is my brother, Zayn Malik."

Cora's tummy fluttered as she looked behind her at the man named Zayn. Lower down, between her thighs, her sex seemed to swell. A woman could come just from the stare of his blue eyed gaze.

"Well, it was very nice to meet you both, but I'm not feeling the best...so, um..."

Cora stumbled forward. A steely arm wrapped around her from behind. Blonde hair lightly dusted the arm roped with muscles upon muscles. Tattoos covered every available inch of skin she could see.

"Easy," Zayn murmured.

Cora blinked. Her stomach twisted; her pulse beat so loud she was sure even the man not holding her could hear it. Why did she feel like something monumental was about to happen?

"What the hell is wrong with me?"

Around her she saw white flashes. More men seemed to fill her once empty clinic. She wasn't a fan of having people witness her in a towel, let alone if she was going to either hump the man holding her or pass out. Either option seemed possible.

She blinked her eyes a few times to clear her vision. The newcomers pushed and jostled or shoved for prime position to see what the action was, making it the last straw for Cora. The equipment, along with all the instruments, was expensive, and not something she wanted to have to replace.

"Everyone stop!" Cora yelled, stepping forward with her hand out, hoping they didn't see the way it shook.

Zayn pulled her in closer to his body, eliminating the small space she'd attempted to put between them for her own peace of mind. Did the man not understand personal space?

Niall inclined his head. "You heard the lady. Everyone move out. The situation is in hand."

"Zayn's got something in hand."

"Watch your tone, McDowell." Niall warned.

McDowell was easily fifty pounds heavier than Niall, and it looked to be all muscle, but he seemed to shrink right before Cora's eyes at Niall's command. Cora studied all the men in front of her with a slow inspection. Faded denim hugged muscular legs, skin tight T-shirts or sleeveless flannel button down covered equally muscular torsos. Each man looked as if he stepped off the cover of some muscle magazine. She may be new to the Mystic River area, but she was pretty sure it was not normal for so many gorgeous men to be in one place, unless...*Oh please don't be gay.*

The extremely large erection digging into her back gave her hope that the man holding her wasn't, but in this day and age one just never knew.

"Sorry, Alpha. We see you found your cub." McDowell nodded towards Niall.

"Yes, let's head back. I'm sure he's tired from his long day."

Cora pulled her attention from checking out the bevy of gorgeous men to see the look of love shining in Niall's eyes as he looked down into the blue eyes of the wolf in his arms.

"Where did you say the trap was, Cora?" Zayn asked.

After she explained where it was located off the running trail, all the men in the room trained their eyes on her. "What are you looking at me like that for?"

"How did you get him back here?" Niall fired the question at her.

"I wrapped him in my jacket, picked him up, and carried him." Her arms still felt like Jell-O from carrying him for over two miles.

"You carried an injured, sixty-five pound cub, over two miles?' Zayn raised his brows.

Cora frowned. "Are you calling me a liar?" She spun out of his arms, nearly falling in her haste. She raised her hand when Zayn reached to touch her. "First of all, he weighs seventy-two pounds." She pointed to the cub in question. "Second of all, I usually run over five miles every day, not to mention I do yoga and cross-fit. So yeah, carrying him was really hard, and I nearly fell several times. My arms hurt just holding them up right now, but I did it, and I would do it again. I am not a liar. You and whoever else who don't believe me can go fuck yourself, and get the hell out of my clinic, because I'm tired, cranky, and I really need to lie down."

"Everybody back the fuck up." Zayn reached for her.

She took a deep breath. There were half a dozen men in the clinic, and she had no clue how they'd gotten in, or why they were all there. "Who are all of you, and why are you here? How did you get in?" The sound of distress from the cub stirred her overprotective instincts.

Forcing herself to turn her attention back to the man who seemed to be in charge, Cora smiled at the wide awake cub. "Did all that ruckus wake you up?"

Cora looked up into blue eyes very similar to the young wolf, but shook off the notion. "He may need some more pain meds. I had him on an IV drip, but *someone* took it out. I can give you some in pill form that you can mix in with his food if you notice him having any discomfort."

"Thank you, Cora. These are men from my...ah...family. When a cub goes missing everyone drops what they're doing to search. I'm sorry if we've scared you." Niall inclined his head.

She flicked away his thank you with a wave of her hand, glad to see almost everyone had cleared out, like they'd been waiting for the order. Now, if she could just get rid of the last of her unwanted visitors, she could go to bed. Surely by the time she woke up in the morning, she'd feel much better. If not, she'd go to the doctor, even if she hated the thought of that.

"Do you have someone to take care of you?" Niall asked.

"I don't need anyone taking care of me."

"I'm afraid I can't leave you here alone, Cora. Either you come home with us, or Zayn stays with you. We owe you a life debt."

"That's...that's crazy. I just saved your pet. Now you have him and everything is fine. I just have a bit of a cold. It's fine."

Niall shook his head, and Zayn's scowl deepened. "Seriously, I'm fine," she repeated.

"You coming with us, or is he staying here?"

He was an immovable obstacle. What do you do with an immovable obstacle? You go around him. Cora was glad her wits were still functioning, even though she knew her fever had to be even higher than the last time she took it.

"How about if I take some meds and call you in the morning?" See, she could be reasonable. She nodded.

"Did you grab her bag?"

With a quick glance, Cora gawked at the sight of Zayn holding her overnight bag with more than just a change of clothing. "Yes," Zayn growled.

"Good. Grab the girl."

What were the chances she could make it down the hall to her apartment with the steel door before either man could catch her? And if she did make it, could she get the alarm set and the police called before she passed out?

All these questions became a moot point when the man in front of her turned on his bare feet, which she just noticed, and walked out the front door, while Zayn murmured next to her ear, "You wouldn't make it two feet before I caught you."

"What?" Her voice came out in a breathless squeak she blamed on fright.

"You have very expressive eyes, and they were saying very clearly that you were about to do a runner. Rest assured, nobody, and I mean nobody in our...home would ever hurt you. We only want to see to your safety and wellbeing."

The last bit of strength Cora possessed left her all at once. Fortunately for her, Zayn just happened to be there to stop her from kissing the floor. Still, common sense told her she should let someone know where she was, just in case they planned to murder her—or something.

"I need to let my assistant know where I am in case of an emergency."

"It's Saturday. Aren't you closed on Sundays?"

Her challenge almost faded on her lips, not because she'd lost her senses, but because he'd bent his head so close to hers she could feel his breath on her lips. For a moment she almost forgot how to breathe. Holy buckets, the man was potent.

"I said in case of an emergency."

"Fine. Who do you need to call?"

Cora swallowed. Surely if they were going to kill her, they wouldn't allow her to let people know where she was going. Right?

With a grunt, Zayn waited while she left a voicemail for her assistant, letting her know she'd be staying with the Maliks and to call her cell if she needed her.

"Okay. You can put me down."

"Not gonna happen. You'll fall down, and then Niall will blame me."

Cora gaped at his audacity. "You can't carry me all the way back to your place."

"One of the guys brought my truck. I only have to carry you out front," he grunted.

She was too tired, and honestly too sick, to argue any further. Besides, his shoulder really felt good to lay her head on. "You smell really, really good."

"You said that before."

Cora closed her eyes against the flashes of white light.

Zayn pulled the door closed, engaging the locks. "Any problems on your way back, Kellen?"

"Coast was clear. Everything okay on your end, boss?" Kellen called from his place against the wall of the clinic.

At the sound of the newcomer's voice, Cora turned her head into Zayn's chest.

"Yes. Thank you for bringing my rig. Can you drive while I hold her? I don't think she will let me go long enough to let me drive us home."

She really wanted to lift her head and give him the finger, but at that very minute she couldn't. The steady rocking from his walk was so soothing her body went lax. Instead of fighting sleep, she let it claim her. A sense of security wrapped around her in the tattooed arms of the big man that she hadn't felt in a long time

Delta Rogue, A SEAL Team Phantom Series

Chapter One

Hailey Ashley looked at the lock on her apartment door, and then at the computer screen again. Ever since the man she'd called friend and team member Dex, had betrayed their team, she'd been living in a state of fear. A game of hide and seek and waiting, until he decided to come and take her out. The other guys were big bad SEALs, while she was the only woman in the group who he would consider an easy target. Until a few weeks ago, she was pretty confident she was as badass as they were. Now, she wasn't so sure. Hell, Blake Anderson was one of the toughest men she knew, and he'd been drugged by the asshole, and taken hostage.

A shudder worked its way through her at the image of the other man lying in the hospital bed. Luckily for him he had JoJo, another SEAL member and his lover. Both men were so in love, she sometimes envied their closeness. "I'm freaking pathetic," she groaned to the empty room.

Thinking back, she wondered how they'd missed the fact Dex had been working for another faction. They all lived in the Steinem apartment building, or at least they had, and hung out regularly. Now, she wasn't sure where Dex was, or Maddox Lopez for that matter. When Dex had shown his true colors and allowed Blake to be kidnapped, then tried to take Alexa Gordon in order to trade her to some unknown person, all so he could make a quick buck, he'd betrayed them all. She was the only one out of the team who'd kept a separate apartment in another location, or at least she thought she was. Now, she questioned everything she'd thought she'd known.

The ringing of her landline startled her, but she let it go to voicemail. More than likely, the same person was calling again. "I don't know anything," she said aloud even though she was alone. Somehow a computerized voice would call her at all hours, demanding answers to questions she didn't have. Her job on the team was not glamorous, or even dangerous. She blended, or if the target was female, then she became the friend and confidante. Hailey drew the line at sleeping with a target.

Tired of staring at the walls, and waiting around to be killed, she unfolded her legs from the sitting position. In a pair of black leggings and a tank top that read *Shut the Fuck up*, she slipped on a pair of tennis shoes, then grabbed her backpack. After making sure her gun was safely inside, she headed toward the door. For weeks she'd hid in her home, only going out to get groceries in broad daylight like a coward. She hadn't seen any of the men she'd gotten used to seeing on a daily basis, the ones she'd called friends. For three years, she lived and worked and had no other friends in South Dakota, thanks to her job. Well, she was not going to sit around and mope, or fret anymore.

Mind made up, she unlocked the deadbolts one at a time, then taking a deep breath, stepped into the hall. The quietness was alarming, but she reassured herself it was normal. She turned back around and relocked the door, then with a press of a button, engaged the security system on her keychain. She may be ready to get out, but she wasn't stupid.

When she didn't encounter a soul in the elevator or the lobby, she exhaled a deep breath. One obstacle down, several more to go. Keeping her head up, and her mind alert, Hailey continued to head toward where she kept her Ducati Monster 696. With her keys palmed, she pulled the helmet off the handle bars, strapped it on, then straddled the bike. The sound of the engine roaring to life made her feel alive for the first time in weeks.

She leaned forward over the gas tank, maneuvering out of the parking spot and headed out of the garage. The sound of a vehicle coming up behind her, set off alarms in her overly tired brain. While she waited for the bar to go up, she looked behind herself and saw a blacked out sedan coming up the ramp. Without a second thought, she eased around the guard rail, and left before whoever was in the vehicle could get within shooting distance. Her fight or flight instinct took over before she could think twice, choosing to run as fast as she could.

The sun going down blazed a bright orange and yellow trail as she gunned the engine, putting much wanted space between her and the vehicle. Swerving between traffic, she tried to picture the license plate, and cursed herself for not paying closer attention. If Mad, or one of the other guys had been there, they'd have made sure to get details, or more than likely, they'd have stayed and confronted whoever was in the vehicle.

As the miles passed, she finally let herself cry for the first time. Tears rolled down her cheeks, and dried from the wind while she drove. Her stomach ached from lack of food, making her decision to get out of the apartment apparent. Another loop up the winding road and she promised herself she'd head back to town for dinner. At the very top, she saw a small roadside area and decided to stop to watch the sunset. With nobody else on the road, the need to take advantage of the perfect moment was too hard to ignore. She hated the thought of heading back to Ohio to her family with her tail between her legs. Sure, they'd hug her and tell her they loved her, but afterward, she would never hear the end of the 'I told you so's', or even worse, 'that girls aren't cut out for that line of work' speeches. No matter how much better of a shot she was than her brothers and cousins, or the fact she could kick their asses in hand to hand, it all came back to the fact, her family believed a woman's place was in the home, taking care of the kids.

The sound of her tires rolling over the gravel echoed around her. She stopped the bike and sat up, cracking her back from being bent over for so long. Taking off the helmet, she shook out her hair, and sat for a few minutes. Pushing the kickstand down, she hopped off and went to stand near the edge of the cliff off to the side. The sound of wildlife like a symphony. Going home shouldn't feel like a prison sentence, dammit.

With a resigned sigh, she turned back toward where she'd left her bike.

Headlights coming up the road highlighted the area, making her scramble to reach the Ducati before they got to where she'd parked. With her heart in her throat, Hailey came to a hard realization, she wasn't going to make it as the large truck pulled in behind her motorcycle. She slipped her backpack off, grabbed her gun out, and trained it on the large man exiting.

Maddox, aka Mad Lopez, rounded the front of his Dodge Ram looking way too good for Hailey's mindset. Dressed in a pair of jeans that molded to his muscular thighs, and a tight white T-shirt, she felt her mouth go dry.

"Nice night for a ride, Hales." Maddox's deep rumble had all her girlie parts standing up and taking notice.

She tilted her head, but didn't lower her weapon. "Why are you here, Mad?"

He shrugged his massive shoulders making her want to run her fingers over his muscles. How the man could keep his white shirts pristine, she had no clue. As the seconds turned to a minute she began to fidget, but refused to say another word.

Taking a step closer to her bike, her thought was to get on it and leave him standing on the side of the road. His dark eyes gleamed as if he already figured out her plans, and was two steps ahead of her.

The sound of another approaching vehicle made Hailey tense. "What the fuck? I swear to all that is holy this is usually a deserted stretch of road at this time of night." No sooner had the words left her mouth, than a spray of bullets pinged the ground in front of her. Maddox shocked her as he sprinted toward her, throwing his body in front of hers, then rolling them both away from their vehicles.

Hailey held her breath, the jarring of the fall somewhat cushioned as she rolled with the man who held her securely in his arms. The closer they got to the edge of the cliff, the more she began to struggle.

"Dammit don't fucking fight me. Those bullets are not fake, Hellion," he grunted.

She almost felt bad, knowing he was taking the brunt of their fall. His nickname for her had always made her smile, yet now she wanted to knee him in the nuts. Since they'd left the hospital, she'd been all alone, thinking about her future. Or wondering when she was going to be taken out. Not once had any of the men she'd been working with had the decency to call and check on her. Of course she understood JoJo and Blake's reasoning, but Maddox was supposed to be her friend. Hell, she thought he cared a little more than that.

Their rolling came to a stop a few feet into the timber with her lying beneath him. Looking up into his dark eyes, she couldn't help but be mesmerized. His lashes were longer than most women, and his unblinking stare made you think he truly could see inside your soul. Only the man was heartless. He'd told her time and time again he didn't do love and forever. She'd told him she didn't do one nighters. They'd come to an agreement that they would be friends and nothing more. However, that didn't mean she didn't fantasize about him on the daily, or nightly.

"Keep looking at me like that and I'll say screw the men pursuing you and fuck you right where you are." Maddox traced a finger along her jaw.

His words made her flinch. Trying for a nonchalance she didn't feel, she smirked. "I was just thinking how incredibly unfair it was you had such girlie lashes, while us women had to put mascara on to achieve the same affect. Now, if you'd get your big ass off me, we should probably be seeing if the fucks who were shooting at *you* are still up there." She gave a hard shove to his chest.

He bent his head a little closer. "Little liar. That's okay though. I'll let you get by with it for now." He shoved up onto his knees. "The vehicle is gone already." Maddox stood, holding his hand out.

Hailey pretended not to notice and scrambled up, standing beside Maddox. At five foot six to his little over six feet, she felt small, especially since he was well over two hundred pounds of pure muscle, and wasn't afraid to show it. "What makes you so sure they aren't parked and waiting for us to come back up?"

Maddox shrugged. "I heard the vehicle as it raced away when several other cars came by. I'm assuming they were hoping to catch you alone."

She narrowed her eyes. "Or, you led them here, or they were following you. Nobody knew I was coming here, not even me, big guy."

A muscle ticked in his jaw. Score one for her.

"Hales, don't push me, okay. I was just coming by to check on you when I saw you fly out of the garage on your little bike. I noticed an SUV following you, but with your *driving*, you lost them. I didn't realize we'd picked up another tail. I'm thinking if we check your bike out, we'd find a tracker on it. Want to test my theory?"

He made it sound like her driving was not up to par, which was absurd. The thought someone had tampered with her Ducati had her hurrying up the hill.

"Slow down, and check your surroundings. Dammit, Hellion, you trying to get yourself killed or what?" Maddox's fingers bit into her arm.

Taking a deep breath she ignored his touch and what it did to her body. "Fine, I'm slowing down, but I want to test your theory." Plus, her backpack and gun had fallen when she'd literally been knocked off her feet as the shooting had begun.

A quick sweep of the area near her bike showed they were alone. She could hear Maddox cursing beneath his breath, but she walked a few more feet toward the sleek bike. Not ten feet away from her Ducati, an explosion knocked her off her feet, sending her flying backward. Again she found herself being covered by Maddox as motorcycle parts flew by them.

"Sonofafuckingbitch," Maddox bit out.

She held onto his shirt with both hands, rolling with him as he took them further away from the fire. Hailey didn't feel any pain until their bodies stopped rolling. A trickle of wetness dripped into her eye. "Oh, god. I never cry, yet I've done it twice today," she whimpered.

Maddox brushed the hair away from her face. "You're going to be okay. Stay calm, Hellion."

Her teeth began to chatter and her body shook. "My bike is gone."

He repeated the same words again as a wave of pain washed over her.

"Don't go to sleep on me, Hales."

"I told the guys you were not into guys. Tired, Mad." Her eyes felt too heavy to keep open, and even though she wanted to stare into his gorgeous face, she let them close having memorized every facet of the man in the last year they'd worked together. JoJo and Blake had teased her mercilessly, saying they were sure he played for their team.

"I most definitely don't swing that way, Hellion," Maddox murmured.

Hailey tried to smile, but the last thought she had was she wished she'd had a chance to find out for sure which team Maddox Lopez played for.

Maddox swore in several languages as Hailey went limp beneath him. The cut above her brow gushed too much blood, making him worry she was going to bleed out on him.

"I need a medic here, stat," he yelled through the line in his ear.

"Man, you're undercover." Mike Royce's voice held a tinge of humor.

"Hailey is fucking bleeding out man. Cut the fucking jokes and get me some help." Maddox gave him their location while he put pressure against the wound. Protocol be damned, he wasn't going to let the woman who had come to mean more to him than she should die on his watch, and politics be damned.

"Shit man, you need to keep calm. Where is the Ice Man?" The tone of Royce's voice had dropped to monotone. Not one Maddox liked to hear aimed at him.

Throwing caution to the wind, he asked again. "You making the call or am I?"

"Two minutes out. What's the story?" All business, Royce didn't say another word.

Staring down, Maddox made up his mind quickly. "Everything stays the same. Whoever blew her bike up was probably working with the ones we are after. If Dex is still alive, he's our line to the assholes. I'm sure they think Hailey and I are weak links since we worked closely with the fuck. More so Hailey since I'm new to the team. We got eyes on Blake and JoJo?" He kept his eyes and ears trained on the road, knowing the assassins could come back at any time. Hell, if it were him, he'd already have come back on foot and have a bead on both their heads.

Royce grunted, which was saying a lot for the other operative. The sound of sirens getting louder pulled his attention away from what he'd do, and on what he needed to do. He could no longer afford to keep hiding behind a façade of SEAL, when the threat was now moved up. Maddox wouldn't allow another woman he cared about to be killed in the line of duty, when he could prevent it. "I'm taking Hailey and myself out of the Steinem Building."

He pulled the earpiece out and stuffed it into his pocket before the ambulance came to a stop followed by the firetruck. A plausible excuse for a perfectly good motorcycle blowing up didn't come readily to his mind, making him realize he was in too deep with the woman.

"What's going on?" the first responder asked, taking in the scene.

Maddox didn't move away as the man and a woman approached with medical equipment. "My fiancée and I stopped here to take in the view, when a vehicle roared past. She and I were walking back toward her bike when I dropped my phone. I stopped to pick it up, but Hailey kept walking. The next thing I know I hear an explosion. Hailey screamed, and I ran to where she landed, throwing my body over hers and rolled to get us away from the falling debris." Maddox took a deep breath, and let it out slowly.

"Sir, we need you to move so we can check her out." The female medic edged around him. "Do you need medical assistance as well?" she asked.

The woman would probably freak if she saw how many scars he had. Instead of answering he shook his head, moving back a little to give them room.

Hailey moaned. "Maddox?"

"I'm here, Hellion." He grabbed her hand as she lifted it in the air, moving into her line of sight. "Lay still while the good medical peeps take a look at you."

"Medical Peeps?" Hailey snorted. "I thought I was the one who hit their head."

Maddox relaxed once he heard Hailey talking and watched as she was strapped onto a stretcher. They stopped the blood flowing from her head, and began the walk back to the ambulance. He glanced at what was left of her Ducati, and warred with going with Hailey, and staying to collect evidence.

"You coming with us to get checked out?" The female asked.

Shit! "I'll follow." He pointed at his vehicle. "Don't want to leave my truck on the side of the road." Half-truths were his specialty. Hell, he was CIA, they practically trained you in the art form of telling what the person wanted or needed to be told, spinning it to where it was believable. His job was to protect the country from terrorists, and the latest threat was from someone on the inside.

"We'll let the ER know to expect you."

He met the too wise gaze of Hailey Ashley, and gave a slight nod of his head. If the cops showed up, one with any sort of training, they would probably find a few stray bullets that would be unexplained, but Maddox wouldn't own up to any of them.

He made sure he had Hailey's bag and gun secured in his possession, before following the flashing lights of the ambulance. The small device was literally burning a hole in his pocket. Shifting his leg, he pulled it out and put it back into his ear. "I'm enroute to the hospital to get checked out, and make sure Hales is okay. You want to hack the computers and clear the way for me. Also, see if there are any hits on the attempt on us today."

Silence met his demands, but he didn't have to wait long before Royce would give him feedback. The ride to the hospital wouldn't take too long, and he hoped like hell the other man at least worked his computer skills to smooth over parts for him.

"Your cover is solid for the medical shit. As for any hits on the girl, or you the SEAL, there's some chatter, but nothing too firm. I'll keep my ears open. You do the same, dick," Royce growled.

"Yeah, I know you love me. Didn't mean to shut you out, but couldn't have you bitching in my ear like an ex-wife or anything." Maddox signaled to follow the ambulance, noticing a familiar vehicle a few cars back. "I got me a tail. Charcoal Tahoe with smoked out windows. I don't see a license plate. He's at the corner of Grant and Ackerman. Can you pull up any cameras in the area?"

The sound of Royce's fingers flying over the keyboard filled the air.

"Got em. There looks like three men inside. Or at least three large figures. One looks like your friend Dex from what I can tell through the camera at the stop light. Dumbasses don't know who they're fucking with," Royce laughed.

Maddox came to a stop near the ER opening, looking behind him. "Are they still following me?"

Royce chuckled. "The light is frozen on red. You got a few extra minutes."

Shaking his head, Maddox parked in the first open spot he could find, then hurried to the bay area he'd seen the ambulance go in, uncaring civilians weren't allowed. He had a badge, one he would pull out if the need arose.

"I owe you one, man." He muttered.

"I'd say your first born, but if they're anything like you, forget it. Alright, they are on the move. I'll watch them through cameras as long as I can, and let you know if there's anything you need to know. Keep me abreast on Hailey's condition," Royce said with a touch of warmth.

His appearance had several paramedics looking his way, but none tried to stop him, making him shake his head. At six foot tall, over two hundred and twenty pounds of solid muscle, most people found him a bit intimidating, especially with his dark looks and bald head.

"Figured you'd be right behind us, but not *right* behind us." The male paramedic who'd shown up on the scene raised his brows as they lifted Hailey down from the back of the ambulance.

Maddox shrugged. "What can I say? I couldn't stand the thought of my girl hurt."

Hailey's eyes widened. "I'm glad you're here, Mad."

"His name is Mad?" The woman asked, pushing the gurney with Hailey on it.

"Maddox Lopez, but my friends call me Mad." He grinned as she looked down at Hailey and winked.

"Well, that is a much better reason than what I was thinking."

"Your friends are circling the hospital," Royce spoke into his ear.

Maddox was used to multitasking. His eyes took in the somewhat busy ER, while he listened to Royce keep him up-to-date on the men following him and Hailey.

Damn! He might need backup. He also should maybe ask for the people's name who'd come to Hailey's rescue, then shook his head. They were probably used to small talk. Maddox, ignored the pang of doubt, and kept the smile on his face.

Once Hailey was pushed inside the small triage room, he went along and kept a close watch. He'd fucked up by not anticipating the attack earlier, which could have cost him and Hailey their lives. Maddox didn't make the same mistake twice.

"You've got that look I've seen before. Right before someone is about to go down." Hailey raised her hand up and mimicked shooting a gun.

The nurse working on getting her vitals laughed, thinking Hailey was making a joke, but Maddox and Hailey knew she was telling the truth.

"Hmm, I can think of all kinds of things I could say, but I don't want to make you blush." His words had the desired effect. Easing the tension from Hailey's body, and making the nurse in the room laugh.

FireStarter, SmokeJumpers Book 1

Keanu Raine walked a few feet from his team, letting his inner fire control him. The forest fire was all but burned out, but it was searching for more, and he knew it had found a new source. The living, breathing entity of unforgiving heat that could engulf hundreds of acres only needed a little spark to ignite all over again, only Keanu wasn't going to allow it if he could stop it. He ignored their questions knowing they were missing something. The hair on the back of his neck stood on end, never a good sign when you were in the middle of a huge forest fire. "Hey, did you guys hear that?" Keanu asked.

"Shit, man, this gobbler is a fuck nut," Brax McKay grumbled.

"Kea, all I can hear is my stomach rumbling." Hal Aldridge grinned, his blond hair soaked with sweat.

"I swear something's not right." Keanu nodded in the direction of the burned out forest.

He couldn't squash the feeling of doom as he looked through the smoke. His inner fire leapt to life, sending his senses on high alert. A small blaze could easily turn into something much larger with the dry conditions, and in Keanu's opinion, it was a guarantee. They'd evacuated the surrounding homes, but it wasn't always a certainty all families would get out.

"I'm going to scout around a bit, since we have about thirty minutes before pick-up. You guys head for the zone and wait for my call. If I'm not there when the DC shows, I'll meet you at the next drop." He tapped the radio attached to his suit.

"Yeah, right, boss. I don't think so, I'm going with you," Hal snorted, moving to stand by him.

"It's cool. I'll go by myself. It's probably nothing." Keanu shrugged.

Hal shook his head. "Let's go."

The group of smokejumpers paused and Keanu nodded to Brax. He knew Hal would follow him regardless. They left the other six members of their team and headed in the direction that Keanu sensed the disturbance. The overwhelming feeling persisted. Someone was trapped in the middle of the blaze. He could feel it in his bones. They needed to locate him or her quickly, or there wouldn't be anything left to find.

Several minutes later, they stood on the outskirts of an already evacuated community. Keanu considered calling a stop to their search, fearing he was too late. There were towering homes to his right, less than a hundred yards away, and blackened earth to his left.

"Kea, if there was someone here, they must've gotten out."

Keanu wasn't sure how Hal knew he was searching for a person, but he had figured out early on Hal was every bit as sensitive as he was.

Hearing Hal mimic his thoughts about their search made his stomach drop. The other man didn't have to add *or they were dead*; nothing could've survived in the middle of the area.

Keanu shook his head, not willing to give up yet. "This way, I know I'm right." Turning toward the trees, he didn't need to check to see if his partner followed.

Burnt wood and grass surrounded them. Inhaling deeply he caught a scent so distinctive it made most people gag.

"My water tank is almost empty. If there's a fire, and I'm not saying there is, maybe we should call for back-up."

"There isn't time. I smell burnt human hair." "Shit," Hal swore.

Keanu led them into a thick clump of charred trees. With all the blackness surrounding him, he couldn't see a thing, but he sensed a hot spot. A tingling deep inside wouldn't let him ignore what he knew was a real threat. He rushed to the area before coming to an abrupt halt. A large section of land filled with tall dry grass had started to smolder.

"What the fuck? How the hell did we miss this?" Hal pointed. "Look." A small boy was nestled in the branches just above the flames.

"Hal, you climb and I'll take care of the fire," Keanu ordered, relieved to see his partner and best friend didn't argue for once.

Stepping over the fallen branches and blackened areas, he inhaled the hot air into his lungs. He continued sucking the flames into his body, relishing the feel of the warmth rushing through his system, while using the water hose attached to his pack to douse the hot spots.

By the time Hal had the boy on the ground, he couldn't sense any more flames. He coughed and gave Hal two thumbs up.

They made their way back to their teammates with the small boy cradled in Hal's big arms.

"What the hell?" Brax eyed the child.

Keanu grabbed a bottle of water from his coworker and chugged, while the rest of the group tended to the boy. His inner flame began to cool with the refreshing fluid and he accepted another bottle gratefully.

"Oh man, Kea. You saved the boy's life." Barry looked from the boy to Keanu. Keanu shook his head. "Nah, I just got lucky. Hal got the kid down." "Bullshit! Good job, Kea." Brax punched his arm.

Praise from his team made Keanu cringe. None of them were ordinary men, far from it, but he hated having attention drawn to him. He looked to the sky, happy to see their pick-up overhead in time to save him from unwanted admiration. They'd radioed ahead, alerting them to the addition. The first man took the child. Keanu was the last to leave the clearing. Giving his inner fire free reign one last time, he made sure they hadn't missed anything else. By the time they finished, he was sure the next team wouldn't have any surprises.

Getting into the DC-3 wasn't nearly as fun as jumping from one, Keanu mused as he was finally lifted up.

Keanu stood on his deck gazing at the openness for as far as his eyes could see. He loved the smell of the mountains, the clean pine scent. It was very similar to his home with his grandparents. He raised his face to the sun, allowing the rays to warm him from the outside as his internal fire warmed the inside. Letting out a deep breath, he turned toward the fire pit in the corner and blew a puff of air on the logs, making them burn.

Smiling, Keanu stepped into his spacious kitchen and grabbed a bottle of beer from the fridge. Closing his eyes in bliss as he twisted off the cap, he tipped his head for a much needed drink. A platter of steaks and two potatoes wrapped in foil were on the counter, ready to be cooked. He grabbed the platter, stepped outside and placed them on the grill, then with another breath of air, the charcoals started to smoke and turn a fiery red.

"Yo, Kea. Where you at?" Hal yelled from inside.

"I'm on the deck. Grab a beer and come on out."

Hal ducked his head, avoiding the doorjamb, and joined Keanu on the deck with two bottles dangling from his fingers. Keanu took a bottle from Hal with a shake of his head.

"Oofta, I so needed this." Hal tipped his bottle to his mouth.

Keanu laughed and flipped the steaks. "Is 'oofta' a real word?"

"Hell yeah, it's real. You can use it for just about any swear word."

Keanu stifled a chuckle. "Thanks, but I think I'll just say 'fuck' at least once in every sentence."

"Why doesn't that surprise me?" "Fuck off." Keanu laughed.

They sat in companionable silence, listening to the birds sing and the wind whistle through the trees. Keanu loved being outside almost as much as he loved women. He swore watching the trees sway was like watching a woman sashay as she led her man to bed.

"So, what did your grandfather want?"

Leave it to Hal to cut to the chase before Keanu was ready to talk about it. His grandfather lived at the top of the Cascades. It was only fifty miles away, but it could be another country.

Keanu shrugged. "Something is spooking him, and if you knew my grandfather, you'd know it was major. He scares the shit out of me and I'm a grown man."

"He didn't give you any hints?"

Keanu looked at the pit and sucked in a breath, making the red coals lose some of their glow, before turning to his best friend. "Nah. He needs my *expertise*." Keanu made air quotes, shrugged, and headed to the grill.

"So, are you looking forward to going home, boss?" Hal asked.

"Yes and no."

"We're going to miss you on the team. Not sure what we'll do without our very own fireman." Hal laughed, his booming voice echoing in the still of the night.

"Real funny. I'm still on call in case of emergency situations, and you know Brax can bend things to his will." Keanu raised his eyebrows. The co-leader of their group had truly amazing and sometimes frightening powers, but Keanu wasn't going to tell him he thought he was great.

The man already had a big head.

Keanu flipped the steaks and checked the potatoes.

"I'm going to miss my own personal barbeque-man." Hal had a frown on his face.

He flipped Hal off. He'd had the ability to make a fire out of air since he was a small boy. By the time he'd turned twelve, he'd learned to breathe the fire back into his body without much cost to himself, other than the need to burn off the energy one way or another.

After graduating from high school he became a fireman for the local fire department. Known as a fire-breather in the world of elementals, Keanu could create a small flame or a large roaring blaze, and in the next breath suck it back into his body. Of course, the larger the fire the more energy he needed to burn afterwards.

As a child, he'd hike for miles and freefall off a cliff into the freezing streams surrounding the Cascades. The adult Keanu found other more pleasurable ways to expel the effects, usually between the thighs of a woman.

"You need some help there, Kea?"

Keanu shook off his thoughts of the past. "Could you grab the salad and dressing out of the fridge?"

"No problem."

Within moments, Keanu had the steaks and potatoes on the table. It always amazed him the way the six foot four blond giant waited until everything was set before digging into his food. He'd slice his steak with exact precision into small cube-like bites, and then stab them with his fork, before chewing each piece several times.

Hal always consumed the meat first, then the carbs, followed by whatever was left, claiming he liked to eat the good stuff first. It amused Keanu to watch him. Being a man who loved his sweets, Keanu would skip the meal and eat dessert first when he could.

"Why are you staring at me like I'm some kind of lab experiment?" Hal asked.

Keanu shook his head, raised his fork and pointed it at his friend. "You are the weirdest eater."

Hal raised his bottle. "I get no complaints from the ladies."

"Thanks for the visual, dude."

Ankles crossed, hands resting over his full belly, Keanu leaned his head on the back of his chair and stared at the darkening sky.

Hal kicked Keanu's feet on the ottoman. With a grunt, Keanu made room for the other man to stretch out his long legs, too.

"Have you ever had the feeling your world was about to get rocked?" Keanu asked without looking at Hal.

"Yep! Every time I take a lady to bed." Hal wagged his eyebrows.

"Shut up, dick," he laughed. "I don't mean like that. Besides, I don't get my world rocked when I fuck a woman, I rock *her* world." Keanu smirked.

"Man, you're so full of it. I heard Cathy calling you all kinds of names and none of them good." Hal punched Keanu's arm.

"Damn, she's one crazy-ass bitch. Seriously though, have you ever gotten a feeling nothing is gonna be the same again?" Keanu brought the conversation back around, avoiding the unwanted reminder of his ex.

Hal bumped his size fourteen feet against Keanu's before answering. He felt like a pussy for voicing his fears.

"I don't discount any mysterious crap. For real, my grandmother used to talk about the berserkers in my family, and how they came back every hundred years or some shit. I'm the first *blond giant* in over ten decades." He gave Keanu a pointed look. "My Nana's words, not mine. Sometimes, when I'm in the middle of a fire, I feel like another person is in my body. Ya know what I mean?" Color spread across Hal's face.

Keanu knew exactly what he meant. Every member of their Smokejumper group had special abilities. Hal was clearly a human wrecking ball. He just hadn't realized Hal wasn't always in control, or didn't feel like it at least. "I think we all feel like that to an extent. Have you talked to the captain about it?"

Hal pinned him with a look brooking no argument. "Nothing to talk about."

They fell silent. Keanu let the quiet of the night soothe his soul. One of the reasons he and Hal were such good friends was because neither man pried into the other's business.

"I'd better get going. You want me to help clean up?" Hal nodded at the dishes on the table.

"Nah, I got it."

"Hey, I owe you for cooking, but I haven't mastered the art of making anything other than
Ramen noodles yet."

Keanu blinked his eyes. "Because you have the poor little boy look down to an art. You bat those baby blues and all the ladies line up to cook for you."

"Well, you just smile that bright cheesy-ass grin and the ladies are lining up to take their panties off for you. I think that trumps my free meals."

Both men laughed at the familiar argument, since neither man lacked for food or companionship.

They were opposite in looks. Keanu had dark hair hanging past his shoulders, dark brown eyes, and topped out at six foot. Hal was built more like a swimmer, and had at least three inches on him. Keanu had the physique of a body builder and spent his off-time working out or participating in extreme sports.

Brax, the co-leader of his team of Smokejumpers, recruited Keanu at twenty-two when he'd made national headlines. Now at thirty-three, he was ready to head home and settle down. Being seven years older than Hal, he considered him like a little brother. As the unofficial leader of the team it was his job to watch over the guys, but he'd taken Hal under his wing. Knowing he'd possibly done his last jump, and he and Hal would no longer be working together, Keanu already missed his friend.

He walked Hal to the door and watched as the big man took the stairs two at a time, before jumping into his oversized four-wheel-drive pickup. Hal waved one big hand out the window before executing a U-turn to leave. Keanu waited until the taillights disappeared down the long drive before going inside. After cleaning up the mess, he shed his clothes and stood under the rainforest-like shower he'd installed on his deck. Sighing, he closed his eyes.

About Elle Boon

Elle Boon lives in Middle-Merica as she likes to say...with her husband, two kids, and a black lab who is more like a small pony. She'd never planned to be a writer, but when life threw her a curve, she swerved with it, since she's athletically challenged. She's known for saying "Bless Your Heart" and dropping lots of F-bombs, but she loves where this new journey has taken her.

She writes what she loves to read, and that is romance, whether it's erotic or paranormal, as long as there is a happily ever after. Her biggest hope is that after readers have read one of her stories, they fall in love with her characters as much as she did. She loves creating new worlds and has more stories just waiting to be written. Elle believes in happily ever afters, and can guarantee you will always get one with her stories.

Connect with Elle online, she loves to hear from you:

www.elleboon.com

https://www.facebook.com/elle.boon

https://www.facebook.com/pages/Elle-Boon-Author/1429718517289545

https://twitter.com/ElleBoon1

https://www.facebook.com/groups/1405756769719931/

https://www.facebook.com/groups/wewroteyourbookboyfriends/

https://www.goodreads.com/author/show/8120085.Elle_Boon

www.elleboon.com/newsletter

Other Books By Elle Boon

Miami Nights
Miami Inferno
Rescuing Miami, Coming Soon
SEAL Team Phantom Series
Delta Salvation
Delta Recon
Delta Rogue
Mission Saving Shayna, Omega Team World
Protecting Teagan, Special Forces World
Wild And Dirty ~A Wild Irish Novella~, Coming April 2017

45474278R00078

Made in the USA
San Bernardino, CA
09 February 2017